Freya Copyright © 2019 by Celeste Barclay. All Rights Reserved.

All rights reserved. No part of this book may be reproduced in any form or by any electronic or mechanical means including information storage and retrieval systems, without permission in writing from the author. The only exception is by a reviewer, who may quote short excerpts in a review.

Cover designed by Lisa Messegee, The Write Designer

This book is a work of fiction. Names, characters, places, and incidents either are products of the author's imagination or are used fictitiously. Any resemblance to actual persons, living or dead, events, or locales is entirely coincidental.

Celeste Barclay
Visit my website at www.celestebarclay.com

Printed in the United States of America

First Printing: June 2019
Celeste Barclay

ISBN-13 978-1-7339004-3-0

This book is dedicated to the men who are brave enough and strong enough to love fiercely independent women.

FREYA

Viking Glory Book Two

Celeste Barclay

VIKING GLORY

Leif, Viking Glory Book One

Freya, Viking Glory Book Two

CHAPTER ONE

"Does he have nothing better to do than stare?" Freya huffed as she and Tyra left the training field.

Freya Ivarsdóttir was a renowned and much feared shieldmaiden and the daughter of a jarl. At twenty-four years old, she had already spent half of her life training and raiding with her Norse tribe.

Tyra looked back over her shoulder and scanned the field of battling Norsemen as they trained. As Freya's best friend, Tyra was used to Freya's sometimes brittle disposition, and she knew when her friend was hiding something. Nothing seemed out of the ordinary. The ongoing skirmishes against their neighbors and the general way of life in the northern Trondelag meant the men and women tasked with defending their tribes trained daily. Tyra watched as they swung axes, swords thrust, and spears hurled. She looked around at the many longhouses that created the perimeter of the homestead. Women stood outside doing laundry, one woman swept dust out her front door, and several people stood around engaged in easy conversation.

"I don't see anyone. Well, maybe a ghost from your past, but he's watched you for years."

"What? No. Wait, what do you mean he's watched me for years?"

"Ever since the two of you a few summers ago--- Well, you know. Skellig's had his eye on you, and I think you broke his heart. I believe he's hoping for more than just a reunion under the furs."

"Never."

"Then who could you have meant?" Tyra smirked before adding in a sing-song voice, "Erik?"

"Who else? The man is a burr I can't seem to pick loose. He's always staring and trying to be charming. He couldn't possibly be any less."

"That's not what the other women are saying."

Freya felt a surge of heat and then a chill pass through her before she swallowed. She would never admit how much a comment like that bothered her. The son of their neighboring ally had been staying in their homestead, in her parents' longhouse, for the past two months. She did not want to admit Tyra was right. Every woman gawked at Erik Rangvaldson, and just about every single woman Freya knew offered some invitation to the man. His height set him apart from everyone but a few. Freya knew from his family's extended stay that his looks favored his mother, but his temperament favored his father. Dark honey blonde hair and piercing blue eyes seemed to follow her everywhere. Despite all the attention he received, Freya rankled at the perverse pleasure he took at taunting and annoying her.

"They're welcome to him," she retorted. Freya tried to look over her shoulder discreetly, but she was not sly enough. Erik was watching the two women walk away, and he had the nerve to wave, then wink.

Tyra could not keep from laughing even though Freya picked up the pace with a huff. The women continued to walk away from the training field and up the hill towards the jarl's longhouse. They were quiet for a moment as they trudged up the hill. It was a short walk, but it gave Freya an opportunity to compose herself.

"Freya," Tyra said in a tone only a childhood friend could get away with. "You're not fooling anyone. Not even yourself."

"What's that supposed to mean?"

"Why waste the energy pretending you're not attracted to him? It's clear Erik's interested in you. He's the son of a jarl and cousin to your sister-in-law. He's a fitting choice for you."

"If I wanted a good tumble and a babe in my belly. But he has no intention of anything more."

Freya swung her long platinum blonde braid back over her shoulder as she adjusted her bow on her shoulder. She caught herself before her nervous habit of jerking her vest more snugly closed got the better of her. Her lithe and well-toned figure was muscular, even more so than her shieldmaiden counterparts, but despite that, she never seemed to be able to hide the ample bosom she inherited from her mother. She was self-conscious and hid it with a faked confidence.

"Is more what you want?"

"I never said I wanted any."

Tyra shook her darker head as they entered Freya's parents' longhouse. They moved through the quiet main room that would later that night fill to bursting with the members of their tribe along with those of Erik's tribe.

The two women made their way to the kitchens where Freya's mother was directing the many thralls and free women who worked in the overheated, crowded space. She smiled as Freya placed her bow in a corner and rolled up her sleeves before washing her hands. She detested touching food with any dirt under her nails. Freya rolled out dough and refused to look at Tyra, who snickered again but let the matter rest. The two women spent the rest of the afternoon assisting the others prepare the evening meal before readying themselves to join the others.

Erik Rangvaldson watched as the most stunning and most frustrating woman he ever met walked towards the jarl's longhouse. He never seemed to be able to tear his attention away from her, and his eyes wandered to wherever she was. Erik knew everyone around him knew of his attraction to Freya. He was even sure she knew, but nothing he did seemed to gain him any favor. He remembered his first encounter with Freya, when he arrived two months earlier to inform his father of troubles at home. Freya had been standing on the docks, and in his hurry to find his father, he did not see her. But it was not long before he heard her. She questioned his actions from the very beginning and had been a test ever since. The more time he spent with her, the more his feelings grew from interest to desire to unrequited love. The past two months had been the sweetest torment he had known since he first discovered his body's reaction to a woman.

"She'll never have you."

Erik ground his teeth. He recognized the voice, and he was tired of hearing it. He looked over at the man who was an admirable warrior but an ever-present naysayer.

"Skellig, you seem to understand her well. Is that why she seeks your company so often?"

"I certainly understood what she wanted when we kept each other warm at night."

Erik's hands fisted before he forced them to relax. He would not show this man just how much it bothered him to know that he and Freya were once lovers.

"But that was years ago, and she has not been back to you since. The cold must not bother her."

"You aren't--"

"Could you two refrain from discussing my sister's private affairs where anyone can hear you?" Leif Ivarrson growled as he approached his new friend and the warrior he respected but did not like. He would never discuss it in the open, but he was glad his sister only spent a moon with Skellig. He did not trust the man around his sister. He suspected there was a violent streak he wanted nowhere near her. He had no interest in having to kill a reliable and fierce warrior, but he would always choose his sister first.

Erik nodded and was glad for a reason to change the subject. Discussing Freya with any other man caused rage to fester within his gut. He never directed his anger at Freya, but at himself and whichever man made the mistake of bringing her up. He was unaccustomed to jealousy but had recognized it from the start.

"Our fathers would have us join them before the meal. There may be new developments." Leif, who resembled Freya and their mother, exchanged a meaningful look with Erik.

"Then we should make ourselves more presentable." Erik nodded to the other man as he and Leif walked toward the bathhouse.

"You shouldn't let him goad you. He does it because he can, and you shouldn't make your feelings so obvious."

"That's quite a statement coming from you after you mooned over my cousin. You still do."

"And she's my wife."

"She wasn't when you met her."

"Fate brought us together. I just thank the gods they did. I will never deny how much I love my wife or how enamored I was with her from the beginning. But she reciprocated my feelings. I can't say the same for you."

"You speak the truth even if it's not what I want to hear."

The men entered the bathhouse and stripped down before soaking in the tubs filled with steaming hot water. Both sighed as the warmth seeped into their aching muscles.

"What do you think our fathers have to say?" Erik looked over at Leif after dunking his head.

"I have no idea, but I can guarantee it's about either our enemy or his brother, if not both."

"That's a given. Do you think any more information has arrived about how our nemesis is financing the mercenaries that now make up his army or where they come from?"

"I don't know, but I hope so. Just as he intends, these skirmishes are wearing down our supplies and our morale. He dances around, showing himself just long enough to cause trouble before retreating. Who does he think he is? The incarnation of Loki? It's tiresome. But he does it on purpose."

"Agreed. I only wish we could discover where his money comes from. You and the others destroyed his homestead and took anyone who survived as a thrall. There was nothing left for him."

"I know that is now a large part of what drives him, but the money! I just wish we could figure out how he is paying for what seems like a never-ending stream of mercenaries."

The men finished scrubbing themselves and moved onto the cold-water soak. The homesteaders built part of the bathhouse over an inlet of the fjord. They eased in, but the cold was breathtaking and kept them from further conversation.

Leif and Erik arrived at the longhouse just as Sigrid, Leif's wife and Erik's cousin, arrived. Leif pulled her in for a passionate kiss, and Erik looked away. He was accustomed to the newlyweds' frequent displays of affection, but they only gave rise to his jealousy again. He longed for that opportunity with Freya.

"Perfect timing, wife."

"Indeed. I need to talk to all of you. Now."

Leif looked down at his petite wife and read her look. Erik recognized it too.

"A vision?" Both men asked at the same time.

"Yes. And a particularly vivid one."

"They seem to grow stronger the further along you are." Leif rubbed his wife's belly.

"True. Please can you stop," she swatted his hand away with a smile. "I need to speak to your father and my uncle. You are a distraction when you do that," she ended on a whisper, but Erik still heard her. He could not help but smile. He was happy for his cousin. She had not had an easy start to life.

Erik spied Freya standing just inside the main room watching Leif and Sigrid. He witnessed her look of longing before their eyes met and the expression snapped away.

Erik seized the opportunity and walked to her.

Freya thought about running. She was withdrawn and quiet while she worked in the kitchen. She heard the conversations floating around her and answered when she had to, but she felt more introspective than usual. Her mind kept jumping back to Erik and the way he made her feel. Memories of them fighting together, back to back, swirled through her mind as other, less scary memories jockeyed for their turn. She thought about the time spent bantering and even arguing. Erik kept her mind sharp. He challenged her in ways no one else did. She thought about the way he often defended her ideas or encouraged her to share her thoughts when the tribal councils met. She found all of her drawn to him—her head, her heart, and her body. The longer she spent getting to know him, the more the traitorous trifecta insisted she was already in love with him.

"Hello, princess."

Freya's lip curled.

"Hello, son of a pig farmer."

"Why must you persist in insulting my father? What has he done to you?" Erik smirked.

Freya shot him a glare as she walked past, but he caught her arm and steered her to a quiet corner.

"Release me before you lose that hand." Freya tried to pull away, but his grip was like a vice even though his hand felt gentle. She could not understand how such a contradiction existed, but part of her did not want him to let go any more than she wanted to admit that. This tug of war between her emotions had been going on the entire time she knew the man. From the day she met him, she felt irresistibly drawn to him, but she fought it with every breath.

"Hush your waspish tongue for just long enough to let me ask you something."

"What?"

Freya breathed in the fresh scent of Erik's hair and skin. Tiny droplets from his damp hair dripped onto his collar. She had an overwhelming curiosity to know what his hair would feel like if she were to run her fingers through it. His touch, his smell, his looks, and even the sound of his voice wreaked havoc on her senses. The only one missing was taste. She almost licked her lips. She chided herself and breathed in as she shut her eyes for a long blink. When she opened them, he was staring at her in a way she did not understand. A way that made a low ache begin in her belly while causing irritation to flare in her mind.

"I'd like to know what Skellig is to you?"

Freya jerked back.

"That is none of your business."

"It is when I sense he wants more than mere friendship and harbors more than respect for you as a warrior."

"It absolutely is not your business. Not what he feels nor what I do."

"So, you welcome his attention?"

"I welcome no one's."

"That much you make obvious, but that doesn't mean it's what you feel. Do you welcome his attentions, Freya?"

Freya's blue-green hazel eyes looked into his ice blue ones, and she saw a determination there that she might admire if it was directed elsewhere.

"Erik, it's none of your business."

"That refrain is getting boring. I'm worried." There. He admitted it, and it made Freya pause.

She unfolded arms she had not realized she crossed.

"Why would it worry you when it's not your concern?"

"You're my friend, and I don't like the way he looks at you."

Freya opened her mouth to retort that he looked at her just as much, but she was not ready for that conversation, and she was aware that he was the second person that day to tell her Skellig stared at her.

"We're friends?"

"I believe so. I would hope so," Erik swallowed as he tried to hide what he thought was a beseeching tone. Freya's lack of surprise made him believe only his ears heard it. "I don't trust him around you."

"He is rarely around me anymore." Freya watched under her lashes as Erik's entire body went rigid for a moment. A reminder of her past with another man made his chest tightened.

"Freya, I'm serious. He doesn't look at you with admiration or even longing. It's something else. I would call it possessiveness. I can't stop you from choosing whomever you want to warm your bed, but I can say I believe he would be a hard man to live with if you took him as your husband. I suspect he would beat you within a moon of your wedding. You may be the jarl's daughter, but he will claim you as his property. No woman deserves that, least of all you. It would kill your spirit if you didn't kill him first."

Freya tried to take in all Erik said. He recognized what she had always sensed and the reason she called off their liaison. She also heard him state how he believed a man should treat a woman, a wife. She also knew he was right that if she ever ended up with a man like Skellig, there was little her position as a jarl's daughter would do to save her. And she would kill any man who attempted to beat her.

Freya took a moment to consider her reaction. Something she rarely did with Erik, but the deep concern she saw in his eyes made her pick her words with more care.

"I do consider you a friend," Freya felt her body sway towards Erik's at that admission, so she pulled back further into the corner. "I already know this about Skellig. I saw hints in the brief time we were together. I can't undo the past, and there is no point in regretting the mistake I made in sharing his bed, but I recognized him for who he is. I will never renew my relationship with him."

Erik nodded. He wanted to ask who she would consider a relationship with, but as tempted as he was, he did not want to hear the answer. He might be a glutton for punishment with his attraction to her, but he was no masochist.

"I learned a good number of things from that brief interlude. The biggest lesson was a jarl's daughter has no business entering a relationship with anyone other than the man she will marry. I keep my dalliances to just that. He is the only man I ever returned to over and over." Freya shook her head before looking up at Erik, but she could not look him in the eye, so instead she focused over his shoulder. "He was the first man to ever pay attention. My father and Leif scared away all the other men. He persisted, and at first, I admired that about him. He said the right things and acted as though he cared. He soothed my fears and made me feel special. But within that moon I suspected he coveted becoming the jarl's son-in-law more than he did me. As the new moon began, I tried to break things off, but he was stubborn. By the end of our time together, I had only been with him twice that second moon. The novelty wore off."

"Freya," Erik breathed, "every man should make you feel worthy. You are special. In every way."

He reached out the back of his fingers to her face, and when she did not flinch, he stroked along her cheekbone before tucking a strand of hair behind her ear.

"I understand why your father and brother were, are, so protective of you. You are a rarity to be protected and cherished. I wouldn't want to ever see you with a man who doesn't realize that."

A lump formed in the back of Freya's throat, and she felt tears prickle behind her eyes. She wanted to flee. She wanted to hide her reaction to his nearness, to his tenderness. But her desire for that nearness and tenderness won. She tilted her head towards his hand, and his palm cupped her cheek.

They stood together as Erik's thumb grazed back and forth over her cheekbone. Freya looked down to see one of her hands found its way to his chest. Her palm rested over the steady beat of his heart, and the heat he generated warmed her arm all the way to the elbow. In that moment, she was ready to relent. She was ready to admit how much she wanted him, and how much she feared he would reject her once he had her.

"If you were mine, I would never use you."

Freya felt a tear form at the corner of her eye, and Erik brushed it away before it could fall.

"There you two are," boomed Ivar.

CHAPTER TWO

Erik and Freya jumped apart like two scalded cats. Freya stepped past Erik with only the briefest of glances.

"What was that about," her father asked as she joined him. "Do I need to speak to him? He isn't trying to pressure you, is he?"

"Not at all. Something concerned him while we were training, but he didn't want to bring it up in front of anyone. He didn't want to embarrass me. He may irritate me to no end, but he is a friend, and I trust him on the battlefield."

Freya moved to stand near Tyra and her cousin Bjorn or rather between them as they glared at one another. It was the excuse she needed to end a conversation with her father she was not sure she could steer.

"Tell your friend she is being unreasonable returning to full training. Does she wish to send herself to Valhalla? Where is the glory in that?" Bjorn huffed.

Tyra had been badly injured shortly after Freya met Erik. Their tribes fought together against their common enemy, Jarl Hakin Hakinsson and his brother Grímr, and during one of the fiercest battles, both Tyra and Bjorn were nearly killed. Tyra took an ax to her chest when she stepped in front of Bjorn to protect him. They were separated from the others and forced to work as a team. Bjorn's arm was broken but it healed quickly compared to Tyra's. Tyra nearly died from loss of blood and then infection.

"I know I'm not healed, and I'm not back to full training. You sound worse than an old woman. You whittle and whine. It's annoying."

"And I didn't slog my way through dead bodies with an injured arm and then tend you for a fortnight just to watch you expire because you can't sit still." Bjorn's voice rose with each word, and he punctuated his declaration with a snarl.

"No one asked you to do all that."

"You ungrateful wench."

Tyra leaned around Freya and laughed at Bjorn.

"A wench gets bedded which is more than I can say for the dry spell I hear you are having."

Freya wanted to laugh so hard she snorted. Instead she stepped forward to keep Bjorn from strangling her best friend.

"My fate is tied to yours since you kept me from being killed, and I kept you alive after someone injured you. I don't want to meet the gods any earlier than they intended just because of your foolhardiness."

"And how many times must I tell you it does not tie your fate to mine? Yours has nothing to do with mine. I have released you of any burden or debt you believe exists."

Freya caught Sigrid's stare as she too tried not to laugh. Sigrid walked over and did nothing to contain her laughter.

"You two are worse than brother and sister," she said with a raised eyebrow.

"We are not," they both replied, and now Freya joined Sigrid's laughter.

"You are. You're worse than Leif and I ever were."

"Sigrid, tell this man our futures are no more linked than a bear and a boar."

"Of course, something links your futures." Bjorn gloated at Sigrid's pronouncement, but it faltered when she continued. "We are all linked as a tribe, and you are both linked with Leif, Freya, and Strian because your lives joined when you were children. Stop sounding like children."

Sigrid moved away from the trio as Freya watched Tyra and Bjorn turn their backs to one another. They had always had an antagonistic relationship even as children. Bjorn resented how long Tyra could outmaneuver him when they trained, and Tyra disliked his arrogance.

There was no more time to talk as everyone moved to their seats for the evening meal. The head table had two more added to accommodate Jarl Ivar's family along with Jarl Rangvald's. Ivar sat in the center with his wife Lena to his left and Freya to the left of her. Further down, Lorna, Erik's mother and Rangvald's wife, sat with the younger four children. To Ivar's right sat Leif then Sigrid followed by Bjorn. The table wrapped around so

Erik and Rangvald sat between their family and Ivar's. There was just enough space for thralls to move about as they served the food and replenished drinks. It was an unusual configuration, but it allowed for conversation.

"Sigrid, Leif mentioned you'd had a vision this afternoon. What have you seen?" Ivar hushed his normally loud voice as he attempted to keep the conversation among the two jarls' families.

"It's not so much what I saw during the vision but what I heard. The men spoke with the same burr as Aunt Lorna. The mercenaries are Scots." Sigrid looked apologetically to her aunt, who Rangvald married when he brought her back to the Trondelag. After his warband raided her home and killed her parents, she had little reason to stay.

"Don't be embarrassed of what you saw, Sigrid. A Highlander can be just as much a bastard as any Norseman. Just remember, we aren't Scots. We're Highlanders." The burr always softened her words even when she smirked at her own husband.

"I am not a bastard, just an arse." Her husband responded around a mouthful of food and a smile. He winked at his wife. "Though she is right. The Scots, or rather Highlanders, make war just as easily as we do. They fight amongst themselves more than they fight us. It's what makes them so easy to raid. Neighbors won't help neighbors."

"We should crush his chances for more warriors." Freya spoke up. She looked around the table, waiting for one of the men to censure her. Instead she saw looks of agreement, and Erik was nodding his head.

"Freya is right. We can't hope to end this until Hakin and Grímr no longer have the resources to keep the fight going. We either convince those working for him to stop, or we force the brothers who plague us to give up." It was Freya's turn to nod her head as Erik spoke, but she stopped short when she realized she was agreeing with him. The conversation before the meal still unsettled her, or rather her body's reaction to Erik's contact frazzled her nerves.

"That is why I will go scout." Freya's pronouncement received the looks of censure she expected.

"Absolutely not," Erik pronounced.

"That's impossible," Ivar spoke over anyone else.

"Hear me out. Leif won't sail without Sigrid, and she's already carrying their first child. Bjorn won't sail without Tyra because he believes she's on death's doorstep and the gods tie their fates. Tyra still isn't recovered enough for the voyage or the fight. And I'm sorry, Strian, but your leg isn't healed enough either. That leaves me."

"It does not. *It leaves me.* I understand the Highlanders better than you do. After all, I grew up with one," Erik argued.

"And I know the way south better than you. You haven't raided in months. I returned from one just two moons ago."

Erik and Freya no longer noticed anyone else at the table as they tried to stare each other down. Neither would relent. Ivar and Rangvald looked at one another and shrugged while Lena and Lorna grinned.

"You may as well let them," Lorna laughed. "Saves time for all of us."

There was no one at the table, except perhaps Erik and Freya, who did not understand Lorna's true meaning.

"You are not going, Freya. This is a mission for only a handful of men. I'm not even taking a full crew."

"I will give you that. It calls for only a handful. Too bad your ego is too large to fit in that group." Freya turned to look at her father. "I will leave the day after tomorrow. It will give me time to ready the supplies, choose my *warriors,*" she shot a glare at Erik for assuming only men could make the trip, "and prepare my smaller boat and horses. I sail in two days at sunrise with the tide."

"Your ship won't be able to accommodate those thralls we may take."

"Of course, it will," Freya cut in. "That's its design. We use it when we sail inland because it's shallower and less noticeable despite being longer. It also has a specially reinforced hull at the stern where the floorboards come up to create storage for prisoners. There is a cage of sorts and extra locks to secure it."

Once again, they glared at one another.

Rangvald nodded at Ivar who announced his decision.

"You both go. In Freya's boat with just the number of warriors you need to manage. Warriors from both tribes. You leave with tomorrow evening's tide. Your purpose is to scout. Only engage if you must."

"I must speak to my warriors now. Excuse me."

Freya stood from the table. She scanned the crowded main room and made her way to five men she knew she could trust to not only fight but to follow her commands without question. They would do more than their fair share of work since they would travel with a diminished crew.

"Sven, Knutr, Gauti, Frode prepare to sail tomorrow. Gauti and Frode tell your wives they sail too. We scout the Scottish coast." Freya turned around, but Skellig stood so close their chests bumped together.

"I'm here. You need not look for me." Skellig's sour breath wafted across Freya's face. He had already imbibed more than his share of mead.

"I wasn't." Freya tried to step around him, but he grasped her arm. Unlike Erik's touch earlier, this one had no gentleness. With a flick of her wrist, she had a blade in her hand against Skellig's ribs. "Let go."

"You know I'm a better warrior than either of the women. You wouldn't need them with me there."

"I don't want you." Freya's words, though quiet, made everyone around them go silent. Everyone knew this standoff was about more than just this voyage.

Despite the knife against his ribs, Skellig's grip tightened. From over Freya's shoulder came a voice she had never been gladder to hear.

"Let her go now, or you die here. You don't manhandle a jarl's daughter. You have no claim to her." Erik's words held weight with their quiet menace.

Skellig released her with a grin.

"We shall resolve this on your return."

Erik stepped forward and pulled Freya back against him. His stance staked his claim before everyone.

"It is resolved." Erik's hushed words carried now that the entire room watched the exchange.

Freya listened as the conversation about her no longer included her. She seethed as both men spoke about her as though she was a spoil of war to claim. The matter was far from resolved.

"You are not coming, and I don't want you. We will not speak of this again." She said to Skellig before shooting daggers from her eyes at Erik as she stepped away from them both.

"Tell your wives to be ready," she shot over her shoulder as she left the main room and made her way to her chamber.

CHAPTER THREE

Erik remained in his spot as the standoff continued without Freya caught between them.

"She made her point clear. Leave her alone."

"So now you've found your bollocks and are claiming her. She didn't stick around or agree. I bet your balls are as blue as your eyes."

"But she also didn't declare before two tribes that she didn't want me."

Skellig lunged forward, but it was Erik's turn to press a blade against him. Except this time Erik pointed the blade just below Skellig's chin where it met his throat.

"I wouldn't," was all Erik said.

"Maybe not here." Skellig smirked before storming out.

Erik refused to look anywhere but straight ahead as he made his way around the tables back to his seat. He wanted to chase after Freya, but he knew he had to wait or there would be even more talk than there already was. The only thing he was unsure of was whether waiting would cool Freya's ire or give it more time to grow.

"Thank you, even if my daughter won't say it. The man is becoming unreasonable. He will not make that mistake again. You are right. You can count it as resolved." Ivar waved to one of his henchmen, who followed Skellig, then he nodded to Erik. "Go to her now. If you wait, you may go to sleep tonight and not awake."

"She would kill me in my sleep?"

"She can be merciful."

The table laughed as Erik left.

Erik exited the longhouse but doubled back around to enter through a rear door. He created a gossip firestorm by intervening as he did, but the moment Skellig touched Freya, he lost any sense of reason other than to get to her side. He was ready to tear Skellig apart right there before everyone. He wanted to roar and beat his chest as he pulled Freya against him. Erik wanted everyone, especially her, to know she was his, and he would always protect what was his. But his rational side knew she was not his, and with that show, she might never be. He would try not to make things worse, so he tried to make it look as though he went outside for some air. Erik did not need a few hundred sets of curious eyes following him as he made his way to Freya's chamber.

Erik did not pause before knocking on her door. He did not have to wait long before it was flung open.

"About time." Freya stood in the doorway with an arm resting against the door and a hand on the door frame. It was clear she had no intention of inviting him in.

"Were you waiting for me?"

"To apologize? Yes."

"Why should I apologize when you should thank me?"

"For what?"

"Is your memory that short? Don't you remember why you stormed out?"

"I didn't storm out, but you are right; you did made me leave."

"I never said I did." Erik grinned as their banter gave him hope. She had not slammed the door in his face.

"If you aren't here to apologize, then good night." Now Freya tried to slam the door shut, but Erik was quick to lean his weight against the door to keep it from closing. He did not push hard enough to move her but enough to slip through. This placed them flush against one another. Freya took a step back, but Erik followed.

"Freya, he had his hand on you."

"I'm aware." She glanced down before she caught herself, and Erik's eyes followed. There was a bruise forming.

He lifted her arm as though it were fragile enough to snap in his hands.

Erik ground his teeth as he tried to calm the sudden spike of heat coursing through him.

"I will not kill him for this, but it is his one chance for error. I will kill him the next time he does anything to threaten or harm you."

"You have no claim. Even if you humiliated me by making everyone else think so. I don't need your help. I can protect myself."

"You wouldn't act the same way if someone did this to Tyra?"

"Of course, I would, but that's because she's my best friend. We have always defended one another." Freya pursed her lips. "And don't think it's because we are women that I would defend her or that we must defend one another. She is like my sister."

"And didn't we agree earlier that we are friends."

"It's different and you know it."

"Maybe I don't."

"Then you're obtuse."

"Explain it then. How is it different for me to defend you?"

"Because I am not your woman. I am no one's woman but my own. You made me look incapable of taking care of myself. On the eve before a voyage where I must captain a ship of warriors who must believe in me. Who must follow me. If I can't handle myself when some arse grabs my arm, how am I supposed to convince others to have faith I can protect them?"

"Or perhaps now people will see we are allies, and we do not fight alone."

"Your cousin married my brother. They can't keep their hands off each other. Believe me, everyone knows we're allied."

Erik looked down at the fiery woman and changed tacks. This was not getting him anywhere. Perhaps a little honesty would calm her. He prayed he was right.

"Maybe I shouldn't have intervened. I do know you can defend yourself. But the sight of him touching you, trying to intimidate you, had me charging across the room before I could stop myself."

Freya sucked in a breath through her nose. Erik admitted more than she ever thought he would, even if he did not say it all aloud. The fight drained from her, and she wanted to accept what she knew he would offer. However, she also did not want to wake alone after he would inevitably slip out in the middle of the night. She did not want to let herself long for something she knew he would not offer. A tumble a time or two was not what her heart could handle. But she could manage graciousness.

"Thank you," her murmured words filled the chamber.

Erik could see a battle playing through her mind. He could read her face even if others did not. He was unsure though of what she was fighting for, or rather against. Like earlier in the evening, he cupped her cheek, and like earlier, she did not pull away. However, this time she did not sink into its warmth.

"We are about to travel together, and danger is unavoidable. I only want you to know you can trust me to always side with you." Erik's breath wafted across her face, and unlike Skellig's, it was not sour. Somehow the mead he drank made it sweet. Once more, her senses flared, and her sense of taste felt left out.

"I do trust you. I may have a sharp tongue and be prickly as a pine cone, but I do trust you, and I will always side with you, too. We shall be formidable partners." She backed away and thrust her arm forward.

Erik looked down at it and wanted to grumble, but he clasped her forearm in a warrior handshake. If this was all she would offer, he would take the crumbs and make it a feast.

The next day passed in a blur as the small crew prepared for departure. Freya spent most of her time with Tyra discussing the route and various eventualities in case of weather. Many people believed Tyra was the daughter of Aegir, the god of the sea. She was the best sailor in their tribe, and her ability to navigate through the most treacherous of water or storm was the stuff of legends. She and her crew always led any expedition, so it felt strange to Freya to know her friend would not be there as her guide.

"Watch the fish as much as you do the horizon. If you can't see any fish swimming alongside the prow, then you have your first warning that either rough water or rough weather lay ahead. If you spot a pod of dolphins, follow them when you can. They will always lead you to safety. If you see puffy clouds, even white ones, look to the horizon, then be wary. A storm is brewing. If the wispy clouds fatten, then expect rain before the day is over."

"I know these things, Tyra. We all do. You have a sixth sense about the water none of us can copy. I wish you could come."

"I do too. But I would only be good for guarding the boat. As much as I don't want to admit it, Bjorn is right. I'm not ready for a full fight. I know you go easy on me in the training yard, and the men are even worse. They barely raise their swords to mine and move like sludge out of fear of hurting me. But I will be ready when you return."

The two women embraced then rolled their maps up. They emerged from Freya's cabin and made their way to the deck. Erik oversaw the loading of supplies and the few horses they would take. With a crew of less than twenty, the boat would sail light and quick in the water. They did not need to take as much food or water as they would if they sailed with a crew of fifty or a hundred. Freya and Tyra disembarked, and Freya said her goodbyes. She sensed Erik moving towards his family and watched as he kissed his mother's cheek and hugged his sisters. His father embraced him, and the two men looked like titans colliding. He and his brothers slapped each other's backs and exchanged laughs before embracing.

Freya tried not to watch, but she admired his closeness to his brothers and sisters. She and Leif were the only children her parents still had. By necessity they were close as children, but their bond was unbreakable as adults. They liked each other's company and respected each other. She was glad to see someone else blessed with what she had. She knew Bjorn, Tyra, and Strian did not have the same relationships that she had with Leif, and it often made her feel for them. Bjorn was her cousin and Leif's best friend, but it still was not quite the same as what she shared with her brother.

"Shall we sail, princess?" Erik's mocking tone had returned, and no trace of their closeness from the day before was present.

Freya was ready to snap her response, but she caught the look in Erik's eyes and realized that he was doing this for her. He was putting distance between them in front of everyone.

"Try not to get in the way."

With a final hug for her mother, Freya dashed up the gangway and called orders. It was not long before they were underway. Freya relished the wind as it lifted the hair from her overheated neck. She held the tiller with confidence as she stood with her feet braced apart. As much as she loved to be home, adventure called to her. The two months of rest was what she needed to appreciate sailing again. When she and the others returned from their last expedition, she was exhausted and coveted time alone to rest and enjoy solitude. She needed a reprieve from being around others and responsible for their wellbeing. The time at home restored her, and now she was ready to venture forth. She scanned the horizon and called an order for the crew to raise the sails as she tacked into the wind. She knew once they were in the open water, the wind would shift to their backs and propel them forward with little effort from her crew. For now, the warriors seated on the benches each had an oar. Her eyes drifted to Erik's back. He had removed his fur pelts despite the cold air, and his tunic already stuck to his skin. The thin layer of fabric did nothing to hide the ripples of his muscles as he maneuvered the oar through the water into the air and then back into the water. She watched the muscles in his forearms as he pressed his oar handle down to pop it out of the water, rolling his wrist to feather the blade just above the water's surface before dropping the oar back into the water. She had seen countless oarsmen make those motions—had even performed them herself—but never had they aroused her as watching Erik did. An ache settled into the pit of her belly, and her breasts felt heavy. She longed to run her hands over his shoulders and back to discover if the muscles were just as taut as she imagined. She wanted to feel his arms wrap around her as she explored his body. Her mouth went dry as she continued to react to the scene Erik created before her eyes. She paid no attention to the other rowers. None of them held her interest the way Erik did.

The loud call of a seagull brought her back to reality. She chided herself for fantasizing when she was supposed to be captaining her ship rather than ogling a man who in equal parts annoyed her and aroused her. Her arousal only annoyed her further.

CHAPTER FOUR

The next three days of sailing were uneventful. They spent much of the time looking out over the open sea. There was nothing in sight but open water and puffy clouds. The time dragged for the entire crew. There were only a few hours here and there where the crew needed to row to keep the boat moving. The North Sea was choppy, and the swells often sprayed water across the crew. Some would sing, while many others had small pieces of wood they whittled into figurines of the gods. They did it more to keep their minds occupied than in tribute. Freya watched the crew and was thankful they were all experienced sailors and warriors. She did not have to worry about any getting sick or becoming anxious over not seeing land. Each member of the crew had made this voyage many times. Erik watched Freya as he always did, but he attempted to be more circumspect since they were in closer quarters. He took to heart Freya's concern that the crew respect and trust her. He would not undermine that, so he rowed when it was his turn and took the tiller when Freya sat to row.

Freya was once again at the tiller and watched the water dial in the bucket to keep them on a western course. She estimated they must be within a day's sail of Orkney.

"Freund!" She called to the young boy who served as a cabin boy, scullery maid, and crow's nest barrelman. He loved to climb, had no fear of heights, and was the only one who could fit in such a cramped space.

"Aye, Captain!" The boy, who could be only ten or eleven summers, scurried to her side.

"Climb up and see what there is to see."

"Aye, aye."

Freya could not help but smile as she watched him clamor up the rope ladder. She loved the job when she was his age, and she would still do it if she were not the captain. Her body was lean enough to still fit even though her legs became cramped.

"You have the makings of a fine sailor there."

Freya tried not to jump. She had not heard Erik approach.

"Freund can be a handful, but he's loyal and hardworking."

Erik chuckled, "I'm sure the boy is. He's in love with you."

Freya frowned and shook her head.

"That's ridiculous."

"It isn't. Maybe it's only puppy love, but he adores you." Erik leaned in to whisper, "you are rather adorable."

"This is a small boat. If you insist upon annoying me, you may find yourself stored in the hull. I don't need to be tripping over you or your loose tongue."

"I can think of a way to keep my tongue busy." Erik chuckled again. They were back to their banter as if nothing transpired between them. More than once.

"I'm sure one of your women would happily oblige."

"My women? I wasn't aware any of them are mine. And there are only three on board. You and the wives of two of the men, so I would say none are mine."

Freya crossed her arms.

"A blind man could see any of the women at home want to be."

Once again, Erik leaned in.

"Would it bother you to know if any had? What if I was to take up an offer from one of them?"

"Do as you want."

"I would, but you won't let me." Erik straightened as Freya gasped. She gripped the tiller once again and looked past his shoulder. Erik knew he was being dismissed, but he was not ready to walk away. "I think it would bother you as much as knowing about Skellig bothers me."

"Don't push me on this, Erik. You won't like my answer." She still refused to look at him again.

"Very well. But I'm not making any other offers or accepting any."

Freya was not sure what to say to that, so she opted for the safety of silence. She watched the horizon as the open water greeted them. She and

Tyra plotted the course, and now Freya kept her eye on the coastal landmarks to be sure she stayed within the safe depths. While this longboat was shallower than most, she could not afford to run aground on a sandbar. Freya tried to make her expression seem focused in hopes Erik would get the message. If he did, he ignored it.

"What is your plan for when we arrive?"

"So, you acknowledge it is my plan we will use."

"I don't recall saying that. I asked what it was. I didn't say we would use it."

"Either way, my ship, my plan."

"That is as illogical as it sounds."

"But it would be simpler."

"That is how you plan your battle strategy? Doing what is simpler?"

"When I'm battling you, yes."

"Freya."

"Erik."

Erik shook his head. Why did this woman have to be so awkward? He knew she was only goading him like he had done to her moments earlier. He knew she was not serious, but it still frustrated him. Once again, he changed his approach.

"I'm simply curious what you consider would be best."

Freya glanced at him for only a bat of her eyelashes, but Erik knew she did not believe his change of tone was more than just another tactic. But she was willing to concede a little since, in truth, they needed to plan. It would not take them long to sail to the closest set of islands, the Shetlands.

"I don't believe Hakin is recruiting from Jarlshof. It's too close, but I would like to sail near the coast. There are several settlements we will see from the boat. If anything looks unusual, we stop. If it all seems normal, we continue. There is a possibility Hakin is recruiting from the Orkneys. That would be my first guess. It's close without being the first place he came across. There are more people so more warriors. They don't consider themselves to be Scots, so they have little allegiance to anyone but their own families. We've settled there long enough that many are part Norse. I think it would be easy for Hakin to recruit there."

Erik was nodding his head, so Freya continued.

"I say we anchor off the coast and row in with the horses. We leave three warriors behind and the rest fan out to ride for a day to scout then return on the second day. We can report back to see if anyone found anything of interest. If nothing is happening there, then we move onto Caithness and the mainland. I believe he will stay towards the eastern side of Scotland. He won't want to spend the time or resources to sail all the way to the Hebrides or to go further inland. He's replenishing his supply of men too quickly for any other options."

"I agree. I think each time we go ashore we scout for a day and then meet in the middle. We can push inland along the coast until we find someone willing to talk or we find the clan who's helping him."

"There's sixteen of us, so we leave either three or four with the boat and then break into fours and ride out or we have one group of five. Either way, we need only ride south, east, and west."

"We keep a group of five, and they ride south. They can cover more area if they need to break off."

"Gauti and his wife stay. They are my best sailors. Leave your best one behind in case they must move the boat in a hurry. Divide the rest of your men."

"You ride with me."

"I do not. You ride to the east, and I ride to the west. We should each lead the smaller teams."

"No, we ride together south. Be realistic, we are more likely to find what we are looking for if we travel inland a little way because we'll cover more ground. If need be, we fan out. We need the larger group headed south. And if we find what we're looking for, which I believe we will, as the leaders, we should be there. It will be our decision what to do next, so we must be there to make it."

"You may be right about the likelihood of finding what we look for if we travel south, but I don't believe you think it's about deciding unless it's to later claim you were the one in charge. That or you don't think I can do it." Freya spat out the words and curled her lip in disgust.

Erik was floored. He stood there stunned by the vitriol that spewed from Freya. He admitted, only to himself, he wanted any chance to spend more time with her, and he wanted to be sure he protected her but claiming the credit or having so little faith in her never crossed his mind. His anger spiked. He stepped forward until they were toe to toe and their noses brushed together.

"I never once thought you couldn't handle this. You are the greatest shieldmaiden I have ever seen. You are worth more than ten men even if your tongue is acid. As for claiming the credit, I couldn't give a horse's arse who gets credit. Let it go to our warriors as it should. This is a team effort, Freya. It's not about only either of us." Erik's voice fell to an ominously low pitch, but Freya did not flinch.

"Good. Just checking."

Erik could have throttled her in that moment and then kissed away the sting.

"You are the singularly most infuriating and beguiling woman I have ever met." Erik straightened to his full height, which was impressive, but Freya still came to his shoulders. He knew he did not intimidate her in the least. Her words proved that.

"I wanted to make sure I could trust you. I don't want you tearing off and doing something thoughtless that gets us all killed just so you can claim the glory."

"Have I ever given you the impression I am that type?"

"Well, no. But I know plenty of men who would."

"I'm not plenty of men. I'm me. You can trust me, Freya. I will never intentionally harm you or put you in danger. Just the opposite." Once again, his voice dropped, but there was a different smolder.

Freya looked into the familiar blue eyes. They rooted her to that spot as warmth suffused her. She felt like she was melting as his stare burned to match his words. She raised her chin in defiance as she tried to regain control of her emotions and the conversation, but all she did was bring her mouth closer to his. It was as though they both froze in time for that moment until each seemed to remember they were standing in front of their crew first bickering and now looking like lovers.

"Very well," she breathed, "we ride together, but we share the decisions."

"Haven't you ever noticed despite how we get there, we always come to the same conclusion. We aren't that very different."

Freya swallowed. She thought the same more than once, but her defenses refused to allow her to voice that thought. Ever.

"I'm not your enemy. I wish you would believe that."

"I know you're not. I--" Freya was uncertain what she wanted to say next. Her subconscious screamed for her to admit her feelings. That she wanted little else than to feel his arms wrap around her every day for the rest of their lives. She wanted nothing more than to fall asleep then wake up next to him until they found each other again in Valhalla. But she was not ready to let her guard down, and she was not sure she ever would be. *More's the pity because I know I'm being ridiculous.* "I just find you antagonistic and egotistical. That's why I questioned you."

"I can't disagree with either of your assessments. But am I really? I may goad you and taunt you, but have you ever seen me like that with anyone else?"

Ice shot through Freya.

"Aren't I the lucky one? I'm the only one on the receiving end of when you're an arse. I'm sure seeing only the charming side of you is why every other woman trails after you like a bitch in heat."

Freya spun around and marched towards her cabin. Erik was on her heels, but he said nothing until they reached her door. She swung the door open but tried to shut it before Erik could follow her in. She knew he was behind her, but as quick as she was, Erik was the same. He slipped in and kicked the door shut before capturing Freya's arm and spinning her around to face him. With three steps he had her back against the door. Their bodies pressed against one another as Erik's arms bracketed her head. His hands itched to roam all over her body, but he kept them in place. Freya knew if she tried to get away, he would never force her to stay. She had no desire to run anymore. They stared at each other before bringing their lips to a hairsbreadth apart.

"I want no other. Ever." Erik's mouth descended onto hers as a conflagration of desire and longing burst between them. Freya wrapped her arms around Erik's neck as her fingers tangled with hair as sleek as she imagined. Erik's arm slipped around her waist as his other hand cupped her jaw. His touch was all it took for Freya to moan into his mouth. His response was both a groan and a hum. Their sounds drove them further and faster. Holding each other was no longer enough. Freya felt Erik's interest the moment his hips pressed against hers, but now she knew his lust ran as deep as hers. His thick length rubbed against her mound as she rocked her hips. Her breasts felt heavier and fuller than they ever had. Her nipples were tight darts abraded by the tunic she wore. They ached for the feel of his calloused hands. As though he could read her mind, which she sometimes thought he could, he kneaded and squeezed them. She became restless with the fabric of her vest and tunic in the way. Her hands fisted in his shirt before they roamed over his chest and down the rocky tiers of his abdomen. She moaned again, and Erik tore his lips away to kiss along her jaw until his tongue flicked her earlobe. Her knees shook as a shock of lust coursed through her and landed deep inside her belly.

"I know." He whispered in her ear. "Don't stop touching me, Freya. Please just don't stop." He knew he was begging, but he was a man drowning, and Freya's touch was his only life preserver. He sucked on her lobe as her hands spread over his back and down his buttocks. They were tight and hard. She felt them flex under her hands as she gripped them to the point she worried she would hurt him, but his hips thrust to meet hers. The iron rod trapped inside his pants rubbed harder, and Freya panted as the friction built a need she recognized.

"Don't stop either. Gods--" she did not make it further as pleasure burst through her, and her body clenched around the release. She could not stop moving against him as a second wave crashed before the first one seemed to ebb.

She reached between them, but he encircled her wrist with his long fingers.

"You don't have to."

Freya looked at him and retreated. Rejection stinging.

"No. Don't do that. Don't shut me out. I'm not rejecting you. How can you still think I ever would? I don't want you to feel you're obligated to reciprocate. Seeing you come apart in my arms was the singularly most magnificent thing I have ever witnessed. I would do it over and over again, but you don't owe me anything." He punctuated his speech with a kiss on her nose. The affection soothed them both. She believed him. That single kiss of endearment reassured her more than if their lips fused again.

"I want to. I want to see the same thing you did." She pushed her hand until she could palm the steel that had just given her relief and pleasure. "I need to touch you."

Erik looked down and saw a desperation he recognized from his own mind just moments ago. He nodded as they kissed again. This time it was slow as they explored and learned what each preferred. Freya's hand ran over him and even with the material of his breeches in the way, she swept her thumb back and forth over his tip. His groan spurred her on to add more pressure to her strokes.

"Freya," his breath tickled her skin before he groaned and thrust into her hand. "Gods, what you do to me. How many times I have dreamed of this."

Freya saw the honesty in his gaze, and she knew he deserved her honesty in return.

"Then we are the same."

Their tongues tangled, and they both admitted more in that kiss than they ever had with their words. Erik could not hold back and no longer wanted to. He felt his release sweep through his cock and explode against her hand. He was grateful for the pants that hid how much came forth. It had been months since he touched a woman, and his hand and picturing Freya came nowhere close to what he had now.

Their foreheads rested against each other as their hearts slowed and their breathing quietened. Erik smoothed the hair away from her face. He was not sure what to do. For the first time in his life, he could not think of the appropriate thing to say. He felt he needed to voice some thought, but he did not want to ruin the moment. Freya's mouth opened as though she would say something, but it closed. Erik drew her back into his arms now they had put some space between them as they recovered. He tucked Freya's head against his shoulder and her arms drew around his waist. They stood together until Freya thought she might fall asleep on her feet. She stroked her hands up and down his back as her mind wandered.

What does this mean? Does he think he's laid claim? Is that what I want? Of course, it is, but am I ready to admit that? I don't know. What if he doesn't want me after that? What if he scratched an itch, and now it's gone? What have I done? I can't bear that thought. That he might not want me anymore. Not when I just gave in.

Erik's own mind bombarded him with doubt. Freya was unlike any woman he knew. She dazzled him and left him in awe. He was unaccustomed to feeling self-conscious or insecure, but he was painfully aware that he was not the only man interested in her.

Was this a mistake? It didn't feel like it. It still doesn't, but will she think it is? Will she reject me? Gods, worse, will she think I took advantage of her? I don't know that I can bear that. If this didn't mean as much to her as it does to me, how will I continue to travel with her? To be so near her when all I want is this. This closeness any and every chance we get.

Freya turned her head and tested the waters with a kiss against his throat. She felt his Adam's apple bobble as he swallowed. He kissed her temple and rested his cheek on her head. The affection between them was a surprise to them both. Neither thought of themselves that way, but neither could think of anything more perfect.

Erik found his nerve. He knew he had to tread with care. He did not want to ruin the moment, and he knew with Freya's mercurial temper, it would be easy to destroy what he felt was a foothold into her heart.

"I wish this moment could last until my last breath." When she did not flinch, tense, or pull away, he felt some reassurance. However, when she did nothing, he was unsure if he should continue. Erik refused to waste the opportunity. "Freya, I don't expect anything of you. I won't lay a claim to you or assume anything from this, but I want you to know everything about this was the truth." Erik held his breath.

Freya pulled back enough to look at him.

"I told the truth, too."

They both knew their actions had screamed, rather than spoke, their feelings.

"I never want someone to claim me." Erik jerked, but she put her hand over his heart. "Wait. Just like you told me not to retreat, hear me out. Claiming me takes my choice away. I want the man I am with, you, to know I come willingly."

Erik wanted to ask what she meant by "the man I'm with." Did she mean whichever man she was with at that moment, or was she willing to consider something more permanent? He did not dare breathe a word.

"Erik, I don't know what to do next. I'm scared."

Those two words showed a vulnerability Erik always knew existed but had doubted she would ever admit.

"Me too."

"I don't want this to ruin things. Truth be told, I like our arguing. If I didn't, I wouldn't engage. I'm scared this will change everything between us, and not for the better."

"We don't have to let it. Nothing must change if you're not ready. I'm just relieved to finally admit to you how I feel."

It petrified Freya to ask what that meant. What did he feel? Lust? Love? It went far beyond friendship.

"It's not just lust if that's what you're wondering."

Freya smiled. He could read her mind.

"Was it only lust for you, Freya?" She was sure she felt his heart lurch as he awaited her answer.

"No."

Erik strained to hear her murmur.

He rested his cheek against her head again and closed his eyes. He would not count this as a victory because he did not consider it a game. He felt it was progress.

"I'll follow your lead, Freya. I never want to take away your choices."

Freya knew if she had not already been in love with Erik, she was now. But old habits would not release their hold on her. She was tentative and not ready to commit. Her brief time with Skellig made her guarded. Her few other interludes jaded her. She wanted more of this with Erik. She needed more before she would voice what she admitted to only herself.

"Thank you." Once again, she leaned back and looked up at Erik. His gaze was soft and vulnerable, not at all what she expected. She wondered if he feared rejection too.

"Freya, I'm serious that I will follow your lead. I won't assume anything. I don't want you to fear I will show up this eve and assume I will share your bed. I don't want you to worry I assume I can claim kisses whenever I want. Don't fear I will no longer consider your ideas in our decisions."

Freya heard a great deal in what he said, and she realized a few things at the same time. She wanted him to claim kisses whenever he wanted, which made no sense since she already said she did not like the word claim. She accepted he respected her both as a woman and as a leader, and it made her feel more self-confident. But before she could say anything, someone knocked on her door.

Freya's eyes widened, and she put her finger to her lips while pointing to the corner behind the door. Erik grinned but shook his head.

"Everyone saw us argue, and they saw me follow you. We've been gone too long," he whispered. "No one will think any less of you."

"That doesn't mean I need to confirm anything. Mine won't think less of me, but I don't know your warriors. Perhaps I shoved you in the hull and threw away the key," she hissed.

Erik claimed a kiss. A quick peck on the cheek before he moved into his designated hiding place. Freya opened the door to find one of her warriors trying to peer past her. She raised an eyebrow, and the man's curiosity died on the spot.

"Freya, we've spotted an inlet where we can anchor. According to Tyra's charts, it is deep enough for us to float on the tide without running aground. It's also close enough to not even need the rafts to get the horses ashore. Do we weigh anchor?"

Freya's stomach clenched. She could not look to Erik for his opinion when only a moment ago he said he would consider hers in their decisions.

"Let me think for a moment, because that may be our best option." She tried to make her face the mask of contemplation. She felt Erik's hand rest on top of the one she had on the back of the door. He squeezed her fingers. She knew it meant he agreed. "Tell Gauti to take us there."

"Aye aye, Captain."

Freya closed the door and rested her forehead against it. Erik gave her the space of three breaths before he pulled her back into his embrace.

"Don't worry until there is a reason to." Erik patted her back then stepped away. "I should go though."

Freya nodded even though she wanted to ask him to stay, to come back that night to share her bed, but she pressed her lips together and stilled her tongue.

CHAPTER FIVE

The crew prepared to disembark just after nightfall. They agreed the cover of night would make them less conspicuous, even if traveling in the dark in an unknown area was not ideal. They would divide into their groups and travel a few hours before making camp. Tyra's maps held true, and after some cajoling, the horses waded to shore. Erik and Freya agreed to leaving Gauti, his wife, and Swen, Erik's best sailor, behind along with Freund, who Freya never intended to take ashore. Erik had to turn away to hide his smile at the boy's crestfallen expression, since he knew all too well the feeling of being left behind by Freya. He respected the boy for accepting Freya's decree without complaint. Once on land, the three groups went their separate ways. Freya and Erik rode in silence with two of Erik's warriors and one of Freya's. They encountered no problems as they headed south, but they also encountered nothing of note. They were all tired and ready to eat by the time Freya called them to a halt and pointed out what she suspected was a clearing among some trees. They said little that night as they ate dried beef strips and settled in for a few hours of sleep. Freya offered to take the first watch. Erik wanted to argue, but only nodded. He laid out Freya's bedroll head to head with his. He wanted her near, but he respected her space.

Freya's hour crawled by as her eyes scanned their surroundings but kept landing back on Erik's sleeping form. She had watched him out of the corner of her eye as he placed their bedrolls near the fire. She smiled to herself that he thought of the same thing she did and placed their bedding near each other but not next to one another.

Her relief came, and she tiptoed to her bedroll only to find Erik watching her.

"I thought you were asleep," she whispered.

"I dozed."

"You should rest while you can. Your turn will come soon enough."

"Would it anger you to know that when we are away from your homestead I only sleep well when I can see you from where I lay?"

Freya thought about her response and decided Erik deserved as much honesty from her as he gave.

"I sleep better when I know you are near. I didn't understand it at first, and I never thought I would tell you this. I've been a light sleeper since I was a child because Leif likes to play tricks on me. I started sleeping better during our first ride out after the attack on your home. I couldn't figure it out. Nothing seemed different until our third mission. You went hunting, but I didn't know it. I couldn't find you before I gave up and went to bed. My sleep was fitful the entire night until I woke to find you standing near me speaking to your father. When I fell back to sleep, it was deep and restful. It scared the shite out of me."

"That's not the effect I hoped for." His white teeth flashed in the firelight.

"Each time I tried to fall asleep not knowing where you were, not knowing you would return, I had nightmares until I knew you were back. Nights when I knew you were safe, I slept like the dead."

"And that's why I never fall asleep until I know you're already well into the land of dreams. I never left to hunt or scout until I could see you were sleeping. I would wait even though I was supposed to have already left."

Freya sighed before sliding one arm out from under her fur and reaching it towards him. Their fingers entwined for only a moment before they let go, but it was enough. There had been too many revelations in one day, and Freya could not keep her eyes open. She drifted off to the crackle of the fire.

Erik watched as Freya's shoulder rose with each breath as she fell deeper asleep. The day had been more than he could have expected. He was used to bickering with Freya, and he enjoyed it. It was the closest she ever let him get. He did not think their banter this morning would lead to their tryst in her cabin, but he would not deny the development encouraged him. Erik knew his feelings for Freya were special. He had been with his fair share of women until he met her. There could be no others now.

He could remember coming ashore at her home after tracking his father to Ivar's homestead. He was focused on telling Rangvald that Hakin had kidnapped Sigrid, so he was not looking around. It did not take him long though to spot Freya. It was as though she was a loadstone to him, and he could not tear himself away. The moment he saw her, she attracted him like opposite magnetic poles. Her looks drew attention from every man, but her acerbic tongue intrigued him. His tastes always ran towards the mild tempered and quiet women, but he knew that was because he liked to keep his liaisons short with few expectations. He avoided women with stronger dispositions because he did not want demands placed upon him. Until Freya. He wished she would demand he commit to her. He wished she would demand they plan a future together.

The past two months had been agony and pleasure rolled into a confusing and frustrating mixture. He knew others saw him following Freya like a lovesick puppy, but he could not overcome his longing to be near her whenever he could. He also admitted to himself that he wanted the other men to know he staked a claim. After their conversation earlier, Erik knew Freya would not appreciate the idea, but he would not allow any man to lure away the woman he wanted. When she was near, he longed to make her laugh, even when it was at his expense. His curiosity got the better of him as he wondered what she would say next to retaliate against his teasing. When they were apart, his eyes scanned for her. He told her the truth when he said he never left until he knew she was safe. Erik kept her within his sight in every battle, and they now fought back to back whenever he could manage it. He trusted her to keep him safe, but he trusted no one else to protect her. The logical side of him realized he bordered on obsession, but his heart screamed at the notion of losing her, to death or to another man. At night and early each morning, he took himself in hand as he pictured her. Sometimes he pictured them making love, but most often it was just an image of Freya as he saw her every day. It was always enough to make him finish far faster than he wanted. Their time in her cabin was more than he imagined. The feel of her in his arms far exceeded what he had dreamed of. Her body was supple and firm as he predicted, and her passions ran as hot as his, but there was a softness to her he suspected few ever saw. His mind turned sour when he wondered if Skellig had seen that side or if their relationship had been purely physical. Erik knew there was more between he and Freya than just lust. If their kisses had not said as much, they both admitted it after. But a flair of jealousy surged through him when he thought about Freya sharing feelings like these with someone else.

Erik looked back at Freya after staring into the fire. He wondered if she harbored feelings for anyone else. He questioned whether her feelings were for him only or was there another man that held her interest too. She did such a fine job pretending she was not interested in him, it made him wonder if she was hiding anything else. He fisted his hands to keep from waking her to ask. Jealousy was an ugly beast that seemed to always have the upper hand.

Freya awoke to Erik returning to his bedroll. She had not heard him get up for his turn at watch, but she heard him now settle back onto the ground. The earliest of the sun's rays were trying to peek over the horizon, and the sky had softened to a deep blue rather than the black of night. Freya looked around the campsite and saw the other warriors were still asleep.

"Erik," she whispered.

He looked over at her and saw doubt in her eyes. He watched her scan the campsite again before she drew back her furs.

"Are you sure?" his heart drummed in his ears.

Her face showed her doubt, but she nodded her head and lifted the furs higher. Erik took his own turn scanning those sleeping around them before he crept to her side. He laid down on his side and pulled the furs over them before looking at Freya. She lay on her side too, and they entwined their legs, but neither made a move for more.

"I just needed you to be closer." Pink flooded her cheeks, and Erik's heart sped up.

"I never thought I would hear you say what I feel."

Freya grinned.

"I never thought I'd admit what I feel."

Erik slid his hand onto her hip and slipped his arm under her head. Erik and Freya came together in a kiss that rivaled their earlier ones, but this one was slow. They took turns exploring one another's mouths as they discovered what each other liked. They forced themselves to stay quiet, but Erik growled when her hand slid over his length. The hand on her hip glided to her backside and squeezed mercilessly. Rather than flinch away, Freya ground her mons against him. They gazed into one another's eyes as the emotions flashed across their faces, at last open for the other to see. They lay like that until they heard some of the others shift as their sleep lightened. Erik kissed her nose before rising. He bent over to tidy his bedroll until his throbbing cock settled enough so that no one else would notice it. It was only moments later that the others stirred. The group of five broke down the camp and ate more dried beef as they rode further south.

It rained much of the day, slowing their pace, but Freya realized it was a gift from the gods when she spotted puffy white smoke rising against the gray of the rainclouds.

"Over there," she pointed. "That's more than just a campfire. That's coming from someone's chimney. Perhaps they know something of Hakin."

"I can't tell from here if it is a single cottage or if it's a settlement, but I agree we should find out. We approach with caution to see what we face before we make contact."

Freya nodded as she wiped the soggy hair from her face. They rode closer to find a large farm with a cottage and stables. No one, not even the cattle, was out in the rain. It looked like a cozy home, and Erik planned to take advantage of that.

"We stop here," he said to the others. "Freya and I will go to the cottage together."

Erik led them to a copse of trees where he dismounted. He pulled two plaids from his saddlebag and handed one to Freya.

"You've seen the way the women wear these, haven't you? You can't look so Norse or they will not say a word."

Freya's eyes ran over his tall build and blond hair before smirking.

"I definitely shouldn't look too Norse." Humor tinged her snarky reply.

Erik scowled before breaking into a wide grin.

"Wife, ye shouldnae speak so to yer mon." Erik sounded like the many men Freya had battled during their raids along the coast. Her eyes widened as she realized that he had no Norse accent when he spoke, but his mother's burr rolled through his words. "Aye lass, I dinna plan to sound like a Norseman either. Now, step beyond that tree and put this on as an arisaid."

Freya giggled then choked as she walked to the tree Erik showed. She never giggled.

It was only a few moments before both Freya and Erik emerged from the trees dressed like locals. It was the first time Freya saw his bare legs, and she felt her eyes lock on his muscular calves as he walked towards her. She saw the muscles of his thighs tauten with each step as his plaid swished. Her throat was dry and a hunger the beef strips could not satisfy filled her belly.

"We ride together," Erik spoke for her ears only. "I will take this opportunity to hold you in my arms because I ache to touch you, but we also need the family to think we are a married couple in need of shelter while we travel. Freya, please don't fight me on anything I say. It'll be best if I do most of the talking. They'll guess at your Norse heritage right away, but I don't want that to keep them from talking. These islanders are tight-lipped people to begin with, but they are more likely to talk to a married couple than a warrior traveling on his own."

"As you wish, husband," Freya purred before turning to hoist herself into the saddle. Erik seized the chance to give her backside a pinch. He mounted behind her, and they nodded to the others before riding out.

Freya settled into Erik's arms and let the horse's swaying gait relax her. It had been years since she shared a saddle with someone other than Tyra or Leif. She remembered the same sense of security from when she was a child and her father took her out to survey their land. Freya shifted and Erik grunted. She felt the evidence of his arousal brush against the cleft of her backside. Freya shifted again, this time on purpose, to feel him as her own arousal spiked. Erik moved the reins into one hand as the other wrapped around her waist. He pulled her against his body and cupped her breast.

"Freya," he hissed, "I'm hard as a damn pike. We want them to believe we're married, but I don't want them to know how much I want to bed you right this minute. Keep that up, and I'll embarrass us both."

Freya caught herself giggling for the second time in less than half an hour. She could not remember the last time she had done that and felt lighthearted. It was a relief to not feel so controlled and rigid. She knew it was Erik because she never felt this way on other missions. Relenting to herself and to Erik about her feelings relieved a burden Freya had not realized was suffocating her.

"Why should I suffer alone?" Her hands gripped his thighs as he continued to knead her breasts. "Erik, they will see my nipples through my tunic if you continue. They might think it's from the cold, but I will know it's because I ache for you."

Heat from lust and once again jealousy surged through him. He pulled her arisaid around her just as they approached the fence that ran around the farm.

"No man is seeing your nipples."

"Not even you?"

Erik pulled the horse to a stop as he angled the animal's body between them and the cottage. He lifted Freya from the saddle and slid her body down his. His mouth was on her in a blaze of desire. She met him with her own need and sucked him into her mouth, but the kiss was over just as quickly as it started when they heard a door open.

"Don't offer what you're not willing to give," Erik warned.

"Don't start what you haven't time to finish."

"What have I unleashed?"

"Far more than you can handle."

A loud voice booming a welcome forced them apart. Erik stepped around and took the horse's bridle as he led Freya forward. He wrapped his arm around her waist but expected she would keep a distance between them. She surprised him when she not only drew closer but wrapped her own arm around his waist.

A large man with a bushy beard down to his chest stepped forward. He was close to their fathers' age and built for the farm work he did.

"This weather isn't fit for man or dog." Freya and Erik knew he was sizing them up, and his comment was not an invitation for them to take shelter.

"Ye have the right of it. We kenned it would rain, but we didnae have time to find shelter before the heavens opened on us." Freya marveled at how Erik sounded with ease like the mainland Highlanders. There was no hint of an accent except for the burr. She found it warmed her in a way that only his kisses did. She leaned her head against his shoulder and closed her eyes. Freya could listen to him forever. She let her mind wander to what it would be like if he sounded like that while he bedded her.

"Your woman looks ready to drop."

Freya's instinct was to stiffen and prove that she was not the weakling he took her for, but she knew it was to their advantage if she could gain his sympathy.

"It's been a long journey for her, but she never complains." Erik squeezed her waist as he kissed the top of her head. Freya was not sure if he meant the affection or if he was pretending for the farmer's sake. "I'm right proud of her, but I would get her out of the rain if I can."

A woman stepped out behind the farmer and took one look at the sodden couple before shooing her husband out of the way.

"The poor lass looks to be ready to keel over, and you're out here chlishmaclavering. Come inside, dearie, before you catch your death. Alistair, show the lad the stables while I get his wife settled." The woman was as squat as she was short, but she had a warm smile and sunny disposition against her husband's stormy expression. The man now known as Alistair showed Erik to the stables.

"If it isnae too much of an inconvenience, I would ask if ma wife and I could bed down in the stables for the night. We'll leave at first light."

The farmer grumbled as he tugged on his greying beard.

"I can't have you stay in the stables if I don't want to hear Hagatha go on all night about how stingy I am. You and your wife can make a spot for yourselves before the fire."

"I thank ye for that. Ma wife is a sturdy sort, but it hasnae been an easy journey even for me." Erik flexed more than he needed to as he unsaddled the horse and removed its bridle, but he felt a need to defend Freya. He did not like anyone thinking less of her, so he would admit to a weakness even as he showed his strength.

"Ye haven't been married long then, have you?"

"Nay. Nae long at all." Erik was quick to finish currying his horse. He wanted to ask the man for information, but he also did not want to be away from Freya long enough for either of them to say something that would not match. Erik was sure the farmer and his wife would discuss them later that night. He did not want them to uncover any contradictions.

"Come along then before you fret."

Erik followed the man inside just as Freya unbraided her hair. She gasped when she saw the two men walk in and tucked it beneath her plaid. Erik had never seen her hair unbraided and loose before. It was a river of spun flax, and his fingers tingled not from the cold but his longing to run them through the thick strands.

"Newlyweds from the look of you," the woman chirped. "Lad, sit by your wife and warm her. She's chilled to the bone. I see her blue fingernails even if she won't admit she's cold."

Erik's eyes darted to Freya's fingers before she could hide them. The woman was right. Freya was cold, and he had not even noticed. He was across the room and had her in his lap before anyone said another word. He held her smaller hands between his as he blew warm air onto them then held them against the heat of his body. Freya watched each of his movements and how he cared for her took her aback. It was as if she were his wife.

"Freya, I mean it," he murmured into her ear. The words were what she needed at that moment, and she sank against him. He encircled her in his arms and rocked absent-mindedly. He wished the older couple would disappear and let him revel in this moment with the woman he undeniably loved.

Alistair pulled his wife into his own arms and gave her a smacking kiss which made Freya sit up.

"He isn't much different than I was."

"Not much different than you still are." Hagatha gave her husband a swat on the backside as she scurried to the cooking area. "I'll have some soup for you in just a wee moment."

"How long have you been married?" Freya asked. The hushed tone helped to hide her accent enough for her burr to pass.

"Oh, onwards of a score and a half years."

"Close to our own parents then."

"Most likely. You look to be about the same age as our son."

Erik stilled. He had seen no evidence of another man who lived there. He was on the defensive in case a younger man should arrive and question their motives for being there. The farmer he was sure he could beat, but he did not want to risk Freya being injured if he had to fight a younger man. Freya tapped her fingers against his chest, and he looked down. Her calm eyes reminded him that Freya would more likely be the one defending him than the other way around. She might not have her sword with her, but he knew she had enough knives stashed on her to kill half a dozen men before she even touched one.

Hagatha returned with two bowls of steaming soup she handed them.

"Mind your tongues. Aye, our son lives on the next farm over. You two look to be about his age."

Erik took the opening that the older lady offered.

"We didnae see any other cottages, so we werenae sure if anyone else lived in the area."

"Not too many people around here. A raid a few years ago killed several families. Those left in these parts are the ones who knew how to fight the Norse. And that's only because our families haven't been on the islands that long ourselves," Alistair explained. "It looks like your wife's family hasnae been here that long either. Where are ye travelling to?"

The man's look bore into Freya, but she was prepared for the questions.

"We're returning from visiting my family in the Shetland." She answered just as softly as before. "We had good news to share with them, so we made what we hoped would be a short journey."

As Freya intended, Hagatha seized on the hint and clapped her hands together.

"When is your babe due?"

Freya almost laughed when Erik choked.

"Still getting used the idea, lad? I doubt you have much more time though your wife is a wee thing."

It was Freya's turn to laugh but it was the notion of anyone calling her wee that had her chuckling.

"Late spring if I've guessed right."

The topic was perfect for distracting Hagatha, but it kept Erik from getting the information he wanted. Freya must have been thinking the same thing.

"We knew it was a risk traveling so close to winter, but we couldn't wait much longer. Not if we didn't want to risk having the babe while we traveled or getting caught by raiders in the spring. Though my parents said there's been a Norseman looking for men." She turned a woeful gaze on Erik before wrapping her arms around him. "It frightened me we might run into him. I wouldn't want this man thinking my husband would make a braw warrior for him."

She turned a radiant smile on the couple before adding in a loud whisper, "I don't share."

Erik knew what she meant, and it had nothing to do with Hakin or the story they were weaving.

"Lass, ye canna be rid of me now, so dinna fash. I amnae leaving yer side." Erik looked into her hazel eyes as he made a vow he hoped she understood. The slight dip of her chin told him she did.

"Eat up before your soup goes cold. You can moon over each other once your belly is full."

Alistair ignored his wife's instructions and directed his questions to Erik.

"I don't believe I caught your names when ye arrived."

"I believe ye're right. My apologies," he tickled Freya, "dinna kill me, Anne, for ma bad manners. I'm Alex Mackay. As Anne said, her family is in the Shetland, but mine is from the mainland as ye can see from our plaid. And from ma accent, too."

Erik had already thought of the names while he was in the stables. He knew he could not use their real ones. Even if Freya's family was supposedly on Shetland and her Norse bloodlines were obvious, he did not need the couple wondering how long her family had supposedly been on the island. Nor did he want them wondering why she was named after a pagan goddess if she was supposed to be Christian, so he chose the most neutral one he could think of. He also needed them to think he was from the Mainland, and Alexander was a common enough name.

"So how did ye come to be on Orkney?" Suspicion darkened Alistair's look.

"Ma sister married a mon from here. We are on our way to them," Erik was quick to answer.

"Spreading the good news of your first babe?"

"Aye, ma sister would skelp me alive if I didna tell her. She is all I have left for family in ma clan, and now she lives on the island."

"You are taking a risk traveling when we've already had our first snow. And as Anne said, there's that Norseman, Hakin, who's been riding across the island like a fool trying to recruit men." Hagatha tutted.

"It's my fault. I begged Alex to let us go."

"And it's ma fault for being too indulgent, but I havenae learned to say nay to ma bonny bride." Erik wanted to steer the conversation back to what Hagatha just revealed. "So, this mon's name is Hakin? Anne's parents hadnae caught a name. They only kenned what a fisherman told them. Sounds like more trouble than he's worth."

"That would be true, but his offer is tempting. Our son took it." Hagatha shook her head. "He's been gone for a moon. Hopefully, the gold promised him is worth risking his neck for a man he owes no allegiance."

Freya looked wide eyed at the couple.

"We hadn't heard anything of him on the mainland or much of him on Shetland. Why would he want Scots or Orcadians to fight for him? Doesn't he have his own men?"

"Seems he's set on revenge. Some jarl burned his home to the ground and stole away his people as thralls. He wants back what someone took from him." Alistair explained. "You can't blame the man."

"I suppose nae," Erik replied even though he seethed. Freya looked up at him but remained quiet. He knew she realized she would tread dangerous ground if she showed too much interest in politics. "If they burned his home to the ground, I wonder how he can finance such a plan."

Erik tried to sound as speculative as he could, but he was not sure if he kept the bitterness from his voice. When neither Hagatha nor Alistair seemed to notice, he felt reassured.

"It seems he has quite a twisted family tree. The wife of his younger brother somehow gained land here. She owns quite a prosperous farm and trades with the mainland. Rather than raid, this Hakin recruited using her connections. The woman, Inga I believe, has a husband tucked away on the mainland recovering from injuries. Apparently, he's in a bad way. Rumors say she is cuckolding her husband with his brother. She's trying to convince Hakin to continue fighting her own brother."

Freya sucked in a breath, and Erik felt her stomach go concave. He did not know how to soothe her without making it obvious. He did not need the couple questioning why such news upset her. Erik's focus on Freya kept his own temper from erupting. They were speaking of his aunt who would wage war against his father. He barely knew the woman, but he remembered her as kind if not standoffish when he was a child. She visited a few times a year and brought gifts, but she always seemed eager to leave. If Inga was financing Hakin's mission, it meant she supported him, and that also meant she had no qualms about Hakin kidnapping Sigrid, her own niece. Erik could not believe the turn of events, and Alistair was right. It was quite a twisted family tree. Inga was supposed to have married Freya's father, but he was in love with Freya's mother. Instead Inga married Grímr, Hakin's younger brother, and carried on an affair with Freya's father's captain of warriors. Inga was the sister of not only his father, Rangvald, but his cousin Sigrid's mother, Signy. He understood Hakin's motives and even Inga's towards Ivar, but he did not understand why she harbored such hate for her own family.

"It all sounds vera complicated," Erik could only muster a few words. "I am glad we havenae encountered this mon. I wouldnae want Anne anywhere near such a person."

Erik did not have to try to make the concern show in his voice, but it was not for the reasons he wanted the older couple to believe. He knew Freya would run Hakin through first then ask questions later. He preferred not to think of Freya fighting even if she was one of the finest warriors he knew. Her hand covered his and their fingers laced together. Both were quiet as they ate their soup. They had much to think about and did not want to pry so much as to make Alistair and Hagatha suspicious.

"It is a wonder she has the land in her own right. You would think it would be her husband's, but our son told us it was hers before he left. He said something about money paid to her when her first marriage fell through. There was also some previous lover who stole for her from the man she was originally supposed to marry." Hagatha shook her head. "You're right that it's all very complicated. Anyway, now you are fed and seem to be dry, I imagine you are ready to settle down for the night. Anne, you still look just as exhausted as you did before. The soup doesn't seem to have revived you much."

"It was delicious, but I am rather tired."

"Then let us get you both some furs and make room before the fire." Hagatha scuttled off while Erik and Alistair moved the table and benches further into the center of the main room. Hagatha returned with blankets and a large fur. She and Freya hurried to make a bed.

"It won't be the most comfortable, but I suspect you shall sleep well with such a braw husband as your pillow." Hagatha chortled as she and Alistair made their way to a room off to the left side of the cottage.

CHAPTER SIX

Once the older couple shut their door, Freya removed the plaid and stood before the fire. She was still cold because her tunic never dried from when the rain soaked it before she put the plaid over it. The contrasting heat from the fire only made her shiver more. Strong hands gripped her shoulders as Erik pulled her back against a wall of muscle.

"You're still soaked," Erik whispered as he turned her to face him. "You should have said something. You could have sat closer to the fire."

"I already said far more than I should have. I didn't want to draw more attention by them seeing how different the stitching on my tunic is from Hagatha's."

"But we told them we just came from Orkney. It wouldn't have come as that much of a surprise you would wear something Norse."

"I know, but I didn't think it was worth the risk having to talk more about a family that doesn't exist that we saw on a make-believe visit."

"You need to take this off, so it can dry before morning."

Freya looked at him as though he had lost his mind.

"I am not sleeping half naked in someone else's home nor in front of you for that matter."

"Afraid you won't be able to control yourself," Erik smirked.

Freya's lips pursed. She did not like that Erik understood her reasons.

"I won't be touching myself, so why would I be unable to control myself?" As soon as the words left her mouth, she knew she misspoke. She snapped her mouth shut before she made any more blunders.

"I would not stop you if you did as long as you let me see." Erik pulled her tight against him, so she would remember the interest she must have felt the entire time she was in his lap. "And you're right. I wouldn't be able to control myself at such a sight. I'm barely able to now."

Freya pulled his head towards her as she arched her back to reach him. She initiated this kiss, and Erik let her take the lead. She teased him as she flicked her tongue across his lips until he opened to her, then she lured him in until she could suck on his tongue. Erik's hands sped down her back until he cupped her backside. He helped her rock against his own moving hips.

"Gods, Freya, I have never wanted any woman the way I want you. I want to touch every part of you, taste what I want you to share with only me."

"Are you staking your claim?" Freya breathed before kissing a searing path along his neck until she nipped at his collar bone.

"No. I'm wishing you would stake yours."

Freya did not know how to respond. She wanted to say yes and that she would claw out any woman's eyes who thought to keep looking at him, but she was not sure what he intended. She could not just be a stop in the night for him before he moved on. It would destroy her to share her heart and her body with him only to watch him walk away. So rather than replying with words, she returned her mouth to his and once again sucked him into her mouth, showing him she would like a taste of him too. A taste of what she wanted him to only share with her.

They made their way to the bedroll, and Freya let Erik slip the soaked tunic over her head. He kneeled to spread it before the fire. When he turned back, Freya's hands cupped her breasts.

"Don't hide from me anymore." Erik begged, and Freya heard the beseeching tone.

Her hands drifted to her sides as she relented.

"I don't want to hide from you anymore," she admitted that much, but not the rest of what she thought. *But I don't want you to break my heart either.*

Erik's touch was reverent as he slid his finger from the dip in her throat down between her breasts. He discovered in her cabin that her breasts were far larger than he imagined. She did well hiding them. His finger grazed over a nipple before circling it until it came to a round point. Erik moved his palm down to her flat belly, and his mind jumped to a picture of her round with their child. He caressed the smoothest skin he ever felt before making his way back up to the other breast. He leaned forward and allowed only the tip of his finger to feather across it until Freya arched and held it in offering to him. Erik needed no other invitation before he swooped in to take as much into his mouth as he could and suckled like a man discovering an oasis. Her skin tasted of honey, and he did not knew how her skin could be so soft. He devoured that breast until she offered him the other.

"I ache in both," she sighed as his mouth latched to her. His large palm covered the nipple that was still wet from his ministrations and kneaded the firm flesh as he continued his feast.

Freya's knees dropped wide, and Erik settled more snugly against her. He had spun his sporran to his back before covering her body with his, but now it frustrated Freya when it kept her from touching his backside. She fumbled for the belt that held his plaid in place knowing it was the only way to get the sporran off. She pulled the belt loose, and it was only Erik's position and body weight that kept the plaid from coming loose too. She dropped the belt beside them and tugged the plaid to his waist as her hands cupped his buttocks. Freya moaned as the muscles flexed beneath her palm each time his hips inched forward and then withdrew.

"I won't risk making love to you in another man's home, but I can bring you pleasure even greater than the last time. Will you let me touch you the way I crave?"

His smell and taste were intoxicating, but even in her haze, his request for permission gave her confidence. He was asking rather than taking, even if the intention was to give. She admired him even more, and her body ached to the point of pain.

"Erik, don't wait."

It was all he needed before his hand disappeared beneath the hem of her arisaid. With no pants or even a tunic in the way, he found her core. He felt the heat radiating from her center and felt himself leak when his fingers encountered the dew on her thighs. Erik nearly spilled when his fingers swept across her seam and were drenched before even entering her. Erik cupped her and pressed the heel of his hand against her bud as his finger plunged inside. He felt her hand cover his as she pushed more of his fingers into her.

"Erik, you won't break anything. I know what I want."

Erik knew she meant she was not fragile, but her words reminded him someone had already broken her maidenhead. Someone else knew her as he wished only he did. It was irrational since he was no virgin either, but his jealousy masked a fear he would not live up to her past.

"What do you want?"

Freya locked her gaze with his.

"I want you inside me. Your cock, not your fingers, but I will settle for those for now."

"For now?"

"You know I've already surrendered my body to you."

Erik's stomach clenched. She had not said she surrendered herself to him, only her body. He longed for more. He longed to have from her what he was ready to offer her.

"Then you shall have whatever you want from me."

Freya gasped, and Erik knew she understood. But before she could say anything more, her body took control from her mind and broke apart. She curled up and buried her head into the crook of his neck to keep from screaming. She could not control the quiet moan that escaped despite her efforts for silence. Freya was frantic to touch him as her mind drove her to find his cock and guide him into her. She yanked up his plaid until she could reach and wrapped her hand around his bare rod. She stroked twice before feeling a drop dribble onto her finger. Freya guided him to her entrance and raised her hips.

Erik ground his teeth. He wanted to surge into her and claim her no matter what he promised earlier. The primitive need to find his release inside her churned through him, but he loved her too much to take what she might regret giving.

"Wait, Freya. If we do this, there is no going back. I will never let another man near you. You will be mine."

Freya paused. It was what Erik did not say that made her stop. He claimed her now and had vaguely offered himself earlier, but he never promised to keep himself to only her. Her pride refused to demand it of him or even ask. If he did not give that pledge willingly, then she did not want to hear it. The thought was a bucket of cold water, and her arousal fizzled. However, she wanted Erik to find the pleasure she had. She shifted away from him, so he was no longer at her entrance. She stroked him as she pulled him in for a kiss. Her fingers fisted in his hair as she worked him until he thrust into her hand. He pulled his mouth away from hers to whisper.

"One day, Freya. One day I will be inside you. We will fly to Valhalla together."

He tensed as his release surged from him, coating her belly with his seed. It was the most intense climax he had ever had. He could only imagine how his cock would feel once he was making love to her. He might not have been inside her, but he was damn sure there was no going back now. Erik had visited the heavens, and he was not willing to leave.

Erik rolled from her but drew her across his chest.

"I would be that pillow Hagatha suggested. Freya, I want to fall asleep to you in my arms and wake the same way. I need to."

Freya's head rested against his shoulder, and her hand roamed mindlessly over his broad chest. She stopped when she heard the last of what Erik said.

"You need to?"

"Yes, need. Freya, when will you come to understand this is no dalliance to me? I wish you wouldn't fear me."

"I don't fear you. I have never feared you. Not even when we argue. I'm just cautious by nature."

Erik snorted.

"You are not cautious by nature. You are a daredevil disguised as a Valkyrie. You only seem cautious around me."

"I don't want to make a choice I'll regret. That is the caution I take."

"I am not Skellig. It doesn't matter at all to be if you are a jarl's daughter or a peasant. I'm not after anything other than you for who you are, not what you are."

"You don't need to be. You're the jarl's son and will one day be a jarl in your own right."

"That's not what I meant, and you know it."

"I can only know what I see, and I am still only watching."

"We both did far more than just watching."

"Erik, I'm not ready." Erik did not like hearing those words, but he welcomed her admission even if he knew she hated giving it.

He lifted her chin until their lips touched.

"Know that I'm in no rush."

Freya nodded once before taking a deep breath and wrapping her arm around his middle. They both were asleep before their next breath.

Erik woke when he heard a rustle coming from the couple's chamber. He realized just as quickly that his arms were empty. His eyes flew open to find Freya seated next to him scrambling to get her tunic on.

"I heard them too," she muttered just in time for the door to open.

"Awake already," Hagatha gave them a suggestive wink.

"We dinna want to inconvenience ye further. Ye have been most gracious hosts."

Erik stood and offered his hand to Freya. She placed hers in his and let him pull her to standing before wrapping her arms around him. She had one dream after another during the night. Some ended with them in a home of their own with children surrounding them, but others ended with her broken and sobbing with him nowhere in sight. She needed the feel of him to anchor her while she was adrift.

Erik sensed something was not right with Freya. She was restless throughout the night but never made a sound. Now she clung to him, so he wrapped his arm around her shoulders and held her against him while he spoke to Alistair.

"We followed that worn path south. Is there aught that might block our way after the storm?"

"There is a stream that may have swelled its banks, but it isn't fast moving. You should still be able to ford it."

"I will send you with some food, so wait here just a moment."

Freya straightened and stepped away from Erik without looking at him.

"That isn't necessary, Hagatha. We would not want to take more than you have already given."

"Don't be ridiculous, lass."

Freya nodded and helped wrap a parcel of meat and cheese with a heel of bread before she and Erik walked to the stables with Alistair.

"I didn't want to say anything in front of Hagatha because I don't want her to worry about our son. Be careful if you encounter Hakin. He is evil. I saw him just before my son left, and I know the type of men who were hired. Alex, keep your bonny bride away from his men and keep yourself hidden before you aren't given a choice about joining him."

"If we take the path south, is it safe? Where is Hakin recruiting now, so we ken to keep a wide berth?"

"Last I heard, he'd left the Orkney for the mainland, but his brother remains here with his wife to heal. He's still got some men out recruiting here though."

"Why would any of the men go with him?" Freya tried to sound naive. "Why would they want to fight a war that isn't theirs?"

"He pays in gold and silver upfront and then promises land if a man can survive the winter."

"What land? Are Orcadian men planning to move to the Trondelag?" Erik pressed.

"He promises them land on the mainland. Some of the men see more opportunity there than staying on this small island."

"But we're not Scots," Freya piped in. "Shetland and Orkney are more Norse than Scots. Why go there rather than back to where we are from?" Freya continued to sound puzzled even though she suspected the reason.

"For the same reason as the Norse settled here. We have land that grows more food than they have back home. We have better weather, though not by much, so life is easier. And there are clans still left to raid."

The last comment was what both Erik and Freya suspected but wanted to hear for themselves. Neither had any qualms about attacking the Scots, but they did not like competition.

"Thank ye for yer hospitality," Erik grasped forearms with Alistair before helping Freya into the saddle.

Erik mounted behind Freya, and they rode out in silence. Erik was not sure if the silence after they were past the fence was a good sign or one of trouble brewing with Freya. He nudged the horse south but doubled back through the trees. He did not have time to ponder before they reached the copse of trees where the other three warriors waited.

"Anything of note out here?" Erik asked after he dismounted. He watched Freya from the corner of his eye, but he knew any offer of help would set him back to the beginning. There was no way she would consider it in front of the others.

"No. Nothing more than rain. Not even the animals were out last night. You?"

"Quite a bit actually," Freya commented. She looked to Erik who tilted his head to show she should go on. "Hakin has been here. Inga has a farm somewhere on the island, and Grímr is here recuperating from his injuries. The farm must make a tidy sum of money to be funding Hakin's army, or there is more happening than the farmer and his wife knew. The farmer believes Hakin has moved onto the mainland, but still has someone here recruiting."

"So, what do you propose we do?"

Freya looked to Erik this time and raised her eyebrows.

"We need to meet back with the others. They will expect us, and I'm curious about what they discovered. Perhaps it was even where Inga's farm lies."

Freya mounted her own horse as the others climbed on theirs. She exchanged a look with Erik. It would seem they both missed sharing a horse.

CHAPTER SEVEN

They rode half the day before they came to the meeting spot. The team that rode west was already waiting, and the team that rode east showed up soon after. They discussed what each group observed or learned. The news the westerly group brought contradicted what Freya and Erik heard. There was a farm, and it was Inga's, but Grímr was not there. He traveled with Hakin to the mainland.

"Then it is not worth staying here unless it is to find Inga." Freya suggested.

"I would agree, but curiosity is getting the better of me. I would like to see how such a farm could be enough to fund Hakin's mercenaries. I would love to ask my dear aunt what makes her do this."

"That may be worth knowing, but we didn't hear where the farm is."

"We did," broke in one of the two shieldmaidens on the voyage. "We heard of a farm when we passed through a village, but we never heard a Norsewoman owns it. We only heard the owner was the secretive sort and was the reason so many of the unwed men turned mercenary."

"What are they paying the men with upfront if they don't get the land until spring? The men could only carry so much gold and silver on them," Erik wondered aloud.

Freya thought for a moment before her jaw set, and Erik saw fury spark in her eyes.

"I can guess. What keeps a man happy? Gold and a satisfied cock. Now I understand why there were so few women left at Hakin's homestead when we burned it to the ground. There were only the old and those with children. There were no women my age. Inga brought all of them here. They must entertain the men or are given to them as bed slaves."

Erik watched the fury settle over her and determination radiated from her unlike anything he saw before. Her anger seemed to pulse through her body. "We look for the farm."

Freya was more furious than she had ever been in her life. She glared at Erik and dared him to contradict her. He wisely nodded. Her mind tumbled with images of women chained to beds as men took their turns. She pictured them being given away as wives or mistresses in return for the men's service. The only thing that gave her any consolation was few men survived the skirmishes against her family and Erik's. There would not be many men returning to claim their prizes.

"Which way?"

"It's not on this main island. It's on the most southern one where no one else lives."

"That would put it closest to the Scots and near the passage taken to get to Skye and the Hebrides." Erik realized. "It's not a farm. They're pirates, and the island is where they hide their bounty."

"That would explain it. We head back to the boat and sail south." Freya barely waited for Erik's agreement before she spun her horse around.

They pushed their horses to make it back to the boat before nightfall. They all wanted to be back on the longboat where they knew they were safer than sleeping in the open. Once on board, Freya was captain once more and the others her crew. Erik knew something still bothered her. The discussion and the long ride had done nothing to quell whatever bothered her. He wanted to question her, but he could not for a multitude of reasons: he needed to row, she needed to concentrate, and she would shut him out if she felt she was being managed. She did not recognize a difference between sympathy and pity, so she wanted none of either.

It was dark by the time Freya handed off the tiller to Gauti. She leaned against the rail as she stared at the stars. The entire day exhausted her. The dreams from the night before haunted her, and she feared they would return. It was the first time she dreamed and remembered while Erik slept nearby.

Perhaps it was sleeping too close to him. Will he always torment my dreams if I sleep with him? I didn't sleep with him. I mean if I sleep next to him. Ugh. I don't even know what I mean. I thought it would be even better than knowing he was on the other side of the campfire. I'll be a wreck if I have another night like the last.

Freya was so absorbed in her own thoughts she did not notice Erik was beside her until she turned and landed with her nose in his chest.

"I wondered if you would ever notice me." He grinned.

"You didn't catch my attention."

"Prickly again, princess?" Erik hoped to lighten her mood by returning to their regular banter, but the look that crossed Freya's face told him banter was the opposite of what she wanted. He nudged her to look out at the water again and covered her hand that laid on the railing with his. From behind them, no one could tell he held her hand. "What's wrong?"

"I'm tired. It's been a long two days and sleeping on the floor didn't agree with me."

"That's not the truth, or least not all of it. You didn't sleep on the floor. You slept on me."

"True enough. You were too bony to make a good bed."

"I was hard as bone, but that isn't what you felt. You seemed quite comfortable cushioned against me."

Freya closed her eyes to center herself, but images from the night before flashed behind her closed lids. She snapped them open and ground her teeth.

"What did you dream about that upset you?"

"Why would you think I dreamed anything?"

"Because you fell asleep curled next to me like a contented kitten and awoke prickly as, well, your usual self. I can only fathom it must have been something you dreamed."

"Can my thoughts not just be my own?"

"My apologies. I wasn't trying to pry. I simply wanted to know if there was anything I could do."

Freya wanted to snap that he could help by promising to be faithful or to walk away if he had no intention of committing to her.

"I dreamed of the coming battle."

"Don't lie Freya. You don't have to share what you don't want to, but don't lie instead."

She turned her head to look at him and saw his earnestness.

"I'm sorry. I said what I thought you wanted to hear."

"That's a first, princess." Erik's other hand slipped over to tickle her ribs. She giggled and shied away but became serious again when she remembered where they were. "Relax. I won't tease you anymore."

Freya closed her eyes again this time to hide the prickle of tears. She wanted him to tease her, but she did not want to lose the respect of her crew. Freya wanted to pull him into her cabin and spend the rest of the night with him buried inside her, but she did not want to wake to discover he had scratched an itch and was ready to move on. She wanted to burrow into his chest and have him hold her like he did when they pretended to be married. She did not want to pretend.

Erik took a deep breath before saying what churned through his mind. Teasing her had been a distraction.

"I rather enjoyed pretending you were my wife. I could get used to holding you whenever I want, and no one would think it odd. I enjoyed falling asleep to you next to me though I hated waking up in a panic when I didn't know where you were."

"You panicked?"

"Of course. One moment I was holding you and falling into the best sleep I have ever had, and the next I was awake with my arms empty. I didn't like it."

"I never would have guessed you didn't like to sleep alone." The sarcasm dripped from Freya, but something about thinking how Erik might normally sleep bothered her.

Erik's brow furrowed as he tried to keep up with Freya's logic.

"I do prefer to sleep alone. That's why having you next to me made it so wonderful. I could get used to it. I want to get used to it."

Freya twisted to look at Erik.

"What are you saying?"

"Something I never intended to on a ship with other ears around to hear me and watch." Erik muttered before straightening to his full height. "I'm saying I've fantasized about you since the day I met you. I've daydreamed of you and spent restless nights craving you. I want you by my side in and out of bed, Freya. I'm tired of hiding how I feel about you. Everyone but you has figured it out. If my mind wasn't so full pining over you, it might embarrass me when people see me trailing after you for any scrap of your attention."

Freya shook her head, but words would not come forward. She swallowed twice before she could say anything.

"You've lusted after me. I suspected as much, and our trysts have proven that. I don't see what's to be embarrassed about, since obviously I am attracted to you too."

Erik drew back and tried to hide the hurt she shot through him by reducing his feelings to something as simple as lust. If it were lust, he could bed her whenever he had time and walk away after. He could not walk away from her. Except for right now. He needed space. He needed to collect himself before he begged.

"It's never been lust." He stepped around her and went to find his men. His heart ached as he tried to join the conversation flowing around him. He overcame the urge to look back at her, but he knew when she retired to her cabin. The cabin where they had first kissed.

Freya could not sleep, so after two hours of staring at her cabin ceiling, she gave up and went onto the deck. She nudged Gauti and told him to find his wife. She took the tiller back and was there when the others rose with the sun. They had made good time, and the bright winter stars made it easy to navigate. The long nights allowed them to travel in the cloak of darkness until they reached the southern isle.

By silent agreement, Erik and Freya avoided one another until it was time to go ashore. Erik felt withdrawn and listless for the first time in years. He had the entire night to contemplate Freya in his sleep. He wondered if she meant more to him than he ever would to her. Perhaps she did not reciprocate his feelings, and maybe it was simple lust for her. Maybe he had convinced himself she had feelings that never existed. The doubt and rejection ate at Erik as he watched her move about the ship as they prepared to anchor. He noticed the dark smudges under her eyes and knew she must have been at the helm most of the night. She smiled and laughed with the others and gave orders when needed, but she seemed subdued. Before they even anchored, Erik led his horse from the hull. The moment they lowered the gangplank, he was at the rail.

"I'll scout." He pulled his horse's bridle to lead the way down the ramp and was wading through the water before anyone could say something.

Freya watched him move further away from the boat and then ride along the beach until it came to a sharp bend, taking him out of sight.

Helga and Alva came to stand on either side of her. She was friendly with the women, but she counted only Sigrid and Tyra as her female friends.

"What happened between you two? You seemed to have made progress, but this morning you both look like you're headed to *hel*." Helga observed.

"Nothing. We have much on our mind, and the cottage was an uncomfortable place to sleep. We are tired."

"Half-truths don't hide the whole truth, Freya." Alva shook her head. "I think you are running from a truth you do not want to see."

"And what might that be?" Freya snapped.

"That man loves you with a fierceness any woman would envy. And you keep rejecting him. I'm surprised his pride keeps bringing him back." Helga jutted her chin in the direction Erik rode. "Perhaps he's done coming back."

"Admit you love him too, Freya, before you miss your opportunity. I disagree with Helga. He will always come back, but you will miss out on what is right before you."

Both women walked away leaving Freya to look at the spot where she last saw Erik. Her pride was not doing much to keep her company. Her fear of a broken heart seemed irrational as she thought about all that Erik had said and done on this journey, when she considered everything that transpired in the time they knew each other. Freya thought about the rumors she heard of women offering themselves to him and what she overheard as they discussed him. She realized she never once heard rumors of him taking any of them to his bed. She never saw or heard a woman gloating about bedding him. Freya considered what Helga and Alva told her, and she knew she longed for what they said to be true. She wanted Erik to love her as much as she loved him, and her fear that he did not was what held her back. That fear might also be what would drive him away. She prayed it was Alva's prediction, not Helga's, that came true.

Freya busied herself examining the maps and charts Tyra gave her. She wanted to prove to the women their comments did not worry her, but when Freund called down from the crow's nest he could see Erik returning, she wanted to jump in the water to meet him. She gripped the table near the tiller that held the various skins with drawings and markings on them until she heard the clatter of his boots and hooves on the plank and then the deck. She dared to look up and found Erik staring at her. He handed off his horse to one of his men and moved towards her. She opened her mouth to apologize, but his serious tone cut her off.

"I've found them. It's near to here. Hakin has turned to piracy. There is nothing close enough to here for them to raid, but I could see boats passing along the other side of the island. A farmhouse with several outbuildings sits upon a cliff. There was activity, but I didn't get close enough to see faces or hear anything. A boat's tied to a dock, but I don't know how many there are to man it. It looks like it's sat there for a while."

Erik fought to keep his voice level and detached. He wanted to share his excitement at his discovery, and he wanted to beg Freya to consider him, and he wanted to shake her until she admitted her feelings too. He did none of those things, instead relaying the impersonal information.

"Did anyone see you? Were you safe?" Freya's questions surprised them both. Erik leaned closer and saw fine lines of tension around her eyes and between her brows.

"You worried about me?"

"Of course," she breathed. She looked around and noticed everyone was studiously finding something to do while appearing to not watch them. She did not care what anyone thought in that moment. Freya grabbed Erik's hand and led him to the door of her cabin. She looked over her shoulder at him before pushing the door open. He followed her in and closed the door with a soft click. Freya turned towards him and did something she had not done since she was five and Leif shoved her into a mud puddle then told her real warriors did not cry in front of others. She burst into tears. Great convulsing, sobbing tears. Erik was by her in an instant, and she fell into his arms. She cried until she had no tears, which all things considered, was only a minute or two, but it was enough for her. She eased away and looked up at him through glassy eyes.

"I feared you'd stop coming back."

Erik furrowed his brow.

"Of course, I was coming back. I only went out to scout." Then what she said registered with him. "What do you mean I'd stop?"

"I keep pushing you away, and I feared you'd had enough. You were so serious and withdrawn. You wouldn't look at me."

"I couldn't. It hurt too much. What you said hurt too much."

"What I said? What did I say? I'll take it back."

"I don't know that you can. Not if you meant it. You said all I felt was lust, and that you were attracted to me, but you never said you felt more. You don't seem to understand that *I* feel more." Erik looked at his feet, and mumbled, "Perhaps you'll never feel more."

"Erik," Freya's heart squeezed so tightly that she rubbed her chest. "If it's not lust, then--"

Erik looked up and saw his own doubts and fears reflected in her eyes. He saw insecurity there too.

"I love you."

There he said it. Freya's eyes opened wide before she launched herself at him. Erik stumbled backwards unprepared for the onslaught of kisses. Freya pressed them back toward the door. It was Erik's turn to be caged against it. He did not mind in the least.

"It's not just lust? It's not just an itch you want to scratch?"

"Is that what you thought? What you think? Freya, for such an amazing warrior, you are not very observant. I love you. Yes, I crave your touch and to join with you, but it's because I want us to be together, and that's how I can show it."

Erik waited for her reaction. His palms were sweating as he waited for her to reject him. He steeled himself for when she said she did not want the same thing. He was positive it was what she would say since she said nothing for so long.

"I love you, too."

Erik did not move.

"Didn't you hear me? I said I love you too."

"I heard, but you took a long time to say it. I mean just now, not in general." Erik swallowed to ease his nervousness. He felt like a child all over again, but this was no child's matter. He wanted to make this woman his wife and build a life together. He wanted it to be with Freya, but only if it was what she desired. "You don't have to say it back."

"What? Why wouldn't I? We are both ready to admit it. Why would I keep hiding it?" She looked at him baffled. "I needed time to work the lump out of my throat and to keep from turning into a raincloud again."

"So, you don't feel obligated to say it?"

"Obligated? After the distance I have tried to keep between us? The amount of times I pushed you away? Obligated is not what I felt at all. Relieved is more like it."

"You thought all I feel is lust?"

"That was my greatest fear."

"That's what you meant about an itch. You feared I would bed you, then be done with you."

"You're the most handsome man I've ever seen. You're not short of women who want you. I worried I was just sport for you, and you would move on once you got what you wanted."

"You talked about these women before. What women, Freya? I was on a fishing boat for the better part of two months, then I met you. I didn't want anyone else after that. The moment I saw you on the dock, I was done looking at other women. I haven't been with a woman since months before I met you."

Freya drew her chin back and looked down.

"Freya, look at me. Why are you hiding?" Erik felt a surge of panic and knew it was envy once again trying to take hold. "I had no claim over you. I still don't."

Erik tried to convince himself that he could not hold it against Freya if she had been with someone since they met. He would not hold it against her, but the pain of thinking about it was crippling. He needed the door behind him to hold him up.

"It's all right if you've been with someone else. More fool was I for not speaking up sooner."

Freya's head jerked up.

"You think I've bedded a man recently? Of course not. For several reasons, but the strongest being you. You have ruined me for any other man. I wasn't hiding something. I was feeling guilty for all the unkind thoughts I've had about several of the women in my tribe. The ones I saw trying to get your attention. The ones I feared you preferred. The ones I assumed you were bedding. They were hateful and spiteful thoughts, and now I have to admit the women didn't deserve them."

"We are quite a pair. I should have known. Skellig is the only man who ever dared brag about being with you, and I haven't heard of you linked with anyone else."

Freya looked to the ceiling and pulled in her lips as she blew out a breath through her nose.

"That's because there's been no one else. Not really. Skellig is the only man I've coupled with. There have been a few others I exchanged kisses with and more, but there is only one man I've been to bed with."

Erik looked incredulous. Freya pulled away and walked across the small room. She crossed her arms and tapped her foot.

"Just what type of whore did you take me for?"

He was on her in a heartbeat. He grasped her arms and held them, pulling her onto her toes.

"Don't ever use that word about yourself. I have never thought that about you, and I would kill any man who called you that."

"Erik, let me go," she murmured as she placed her hands over his heart.

"I won't say it again. I thought you were saying you assumed I was loose."

"Not loose. I know that about you. I'm just surprised since you could have any man you choose." It was Freya's turn to look stunned, and Erik could not help but laugh. "You do realize, don't you, that every man under two score in your tribe and now mine wants to catch your eye."

"That's ridiculous."

"It isn't. That's why I feared you wouldn't feel the same about me. That you had your eye on someone else or would find someone better. You can have your pick."

"You were afraid?"

"Petrified."

Freya covered her mouth to squelch her laughter, but it spilled out.

"I don't find my insecurities to be something to laugh about."

If Freya's unfettered laugh did not sound like bells to him and her smile was not so radiant, her lack of concern for his feelings might have insulted him.

"I know I shouldn't laugh, but I can't picture a man like you being insecure about anything, let alone competition from another man."

"This wasn't just any competition. This is about you, and me spending my life with you. It was agony watching you spar with the other men and watching you mingle amongst the men who have known you and undoubtedly loved you your entire life. Every evening meal I watched you enter with another man, I feared that would be the night Ivar announced your betrothal to someone else. Every time I saw a man watching the way you walk or as you bent over, any time one tried to see down your tunic, I wanted to gouge his eyes out. But I feared you might welcome his attention, which would only make me a fool. I know you're oblivious to all of this, but I wasn't. And it scared me that one day you would pick someone other than me."

Freya snaked her arms around his neck and pressed her body against his. She ran her fingers through his hair as she breathed in his scent. She listened to the even sound of his breath as it caressed her cheeks and nose. Before she would taste him, she would admit her own realizations.

"I told you already that I worried I was nothing more than a passing fancy, and I hated the thought of you with someone else. That's why I wouldn't let you near me. I feared that, too. I feared I would let you in only to watch you walk away. I couldn't have survived that. It wasn't until today I realized I entirely concocted my fear. I've never heard any rumors of you with another woman, and no woman has bragged of warming your bed. And I can assure you, any woman who did would not do so in silence. It dawned on me you had not been with anyone else. Not since arriving at our settlement. By the time I pieced it together, you were out scouting, and I feared I'd pushed you away one too many times."

"Princess, you can never push me away one too many times. I will always come back. I'm surprised you didn't hear the rumors about the fool I was making of myself trailing you like a love-starved kitten. I'm no better than Freund."

Freya tugged his hair.

"But you won't be a love-starved kitten tonight because you are the man I will bed."

Erik reached back and unhooked her hands.

"No. That's not enough for me. I don't want you to just bed me. I want to make love to you knowing you'll be my wife. This will never be about just bed sport. I need to know you want what I do. I want to marry you."

Freya shook her hands loose of Erik's grip and tangled them into his hair again.

"Of course, I'm going to marry you. I wouldn't let you into my bed if I weren't. And if you ever think to leave it, to lay your head," she ground her mound against his thickened rod, "or your cock anywhere else, I simply won't let you. You might not want to say you lay claim, which you don't need to because I come willingly, but I damn well lay claim to you. You are mine."

"Always, my love. Always have been and always will be."

They sealed their agreement with a heated kiss, but the boat listed making them stumble. It was the reminder they needed that they could not finish their plans until later. They needed to plan their next course of action.

CHAPTER EIGHT

As night fell, they once again went ashore, this time only leaving one of Erik's men to guard the longboat. Erik explained that it would be easier to go on foot despite the length of the walk. They would be inconspicuous if they slipped along the rock face on their bellies rather than seated on a horse. Clouds blocked the moon and stars that night, and a light drizzle fell. Freya considered it a good sign. They were less likely to run into anyone before they were ready. They crept until Helga spotted an opening in the rockface. They switched directions and moved to the cave entrance. They ran their hands along the walls until someone found a torch in a wall sconce. Erik pulled his flint from his pocket and struck it several times before the fire took and the torch illuminated the cave. The sight before them was like the stories their parents told them as children. Someone filled the cave with chests and there were open crates with gold and silver piled inside. There was more hidden in the cave than any of them had ever seen come from a raid or a voyage. It was clear someone had been stockpiling for a while or had many people to help pillage. Freya lifted the lid of one chest after another to find jewels, cloth, and golden church items thrown into each. Erik counted eight chests by the time Freya finished.

"This explains how Hakin is paying for his mercenaries, but it doesn't give us any clue to who he is stealing from. I still don't think he is stealing from any of the clans on the mainland. He wouldn't if he wanted to recruit from them, too. I believe he's intercepting cargo and raiding monasteries." Erik ran a piece of velvet across his fingers. He wondered what Freya would look like garbed in such fabric.

"I think it's time to intervene. We can't let this stay here. Our mission might have been to scout, but we did, and we found something. If we leave this here, Hakin will keep buying himself mercenaries." Freya looked to Erik. "We need to take this back to the boat."

"Thankfully, the incline isn't too steep. We can carry these back down without too much effort. We must make more than one trip, but we can get most in the first one."

With fifteen of them, the men carried out six chests while each of the women carried a crate. They deposited their loot at the bottom of the slope before going back for the second round. Once everything was out of the cave, Erik waded back to the boat. He and the warrior left behind each rowed a skiff to shore. They loaded the skiffs until they were close to sinking and the rest of the group walked alongside. It was more difficult getting everything up the steep gangplank than it was getting it out of the cave. Despite the effort needed, they finished in less than two hours. They made their way back to shore for a second time and ascended the rock face until they could see the buildings Erik reported earlier. There was light glowing within the main cottage, but everything else was dark.

"Do you have any idea which building the men sleep in? I doubt it's the cottage."

"From what I saw earlier, most are in that large building to the right."

Freya looked around before suggesting they search the building Erik pointed out first. The others agreed with her reasoning. If that was where most of the men slept, then that's where they needed to start. As they came within a few yards, each warrior pulled out their sword. A few of the men carried knives too. The three women all preferred the longer reach and greater surface area of a battle axe.

"We fight back to back," Freya whispered just before they rushed forward.

"There was never another option," Erik grinned.

One of Freya's men went first to ease the door open. When there was no sound from the door or from any occupants, they moved forward. It made their task easy. Most of the occupants were passed out drunk with jugs lying about. The few able to rouse themselves put up little fight. They swept through and left no survivors with not a peep made.

"That was too easy." It did not sit well with Erik that no one put up a fight, and no one tried to sound an alarm.

They moved on to the main cottage after sweeping the other buildings to find they were empty storage spaces. They eased through the cottage door but stopped once they were inside. Not a one of the hardened warriors could believe their eyes. Freya wanted to wretch, and Erik thought his temple would explode from the blood that pulsed beside his eye. There were women scattered about the room in various states of undress, each tied to a ring in the floor or wall. The chamber stunk of waste and bodily odors. Several of the women had been beaten, and they could see their injuries from across the room.

Freya pushed the men back through the door. Baffled, they allowed the captain to order them out. She was the last one back outside.

"Stay here. Do not enter unless we call to you. If those women wake to find twelve Norsemen staring at them, they will scream bloody murder and bring whomever is running this place to them before we can either get them out or kill the person responsible."

"You're not going in there alone," Erik challenged her.

She frowned, "I never planned to. Helga and Alva will come with me."

"I knew that, but that's still not enough in case the women retaliate."

"They're in no position to, and I didn't see a single one that could match any of us. Erik, trust me."

He did not want to agree. He did not trust the women inside, but he would not let Freya think he doubted her.

"The door remains open. We enter the moment we think there is danger."

Freya, Helga, and Alva slipped back inside and untied the women. The three exchanged looks of disgust and horror as they got closer views of the women's conditions. They knew their tribe, and Erik's too, were not typical. Ivar would not stand for any of his men taking advantage of women. His mother died during an attack on the homestead when he was a child, and he witnessed her being raped before the man slit her throat. He refused to allow any woman to suffer as his mother did, no matter where she was from. Freya suspected Rangvald had a similar rule, because none of Erik's men made a move forward, and each looked as horrified as Erik did. Freya knew Rangvald rescued Erik's mother, Lorna, during a raid that killed her parents. He protected her from becoming his older brother's thrall. Freya felt no satisfaction in having predicted they would find women being held as bed slaves. She just never expected the condition they found the women living in.

They terrified the women as they awoke to three Norsewomen moving through the room with knives in their hands, but soon they realized they were being set free.

"Go outside. There are men there, but they are with us. They will be sure you are safe."

Freya caught a woman's arm who looked about her age.

"This is Hakin's hideaway, isn't it?"

"How did you know? Who are you?"

"I am Freya Ivarsdóttir. You will find Erik Rangvaldson outside."

The woman tried to back away. It was obvious she knew the names.

"Wait. We have no intention of harming you. If we did, you would not be walking away. I need to know the last time he was here. Are Grímr or Inga here?"

"No, none of them have been here in weeks. They left us to the men." The woman shuddered.

"They will never harm you again. Go now with the others." Freya watched her walk through the door before she made her way to two chambers off to the side. She did not trust the woman, but she hoped her information was true. Helga and Alva came to her side as they cleared one room then the next. Freya climbed the ladder to the attic but shook her head when she saw it was empty. The two downstairs chambers had men and women's clothing, but nothing more. There were no personal items to say who occupied them or how long ago they were there.

The women rejoined Erik and the others. Freya surveyed the group of shivering and filthy women. She felt sorry for them, but she did not look forward to having them aboard her longboat. She did not want to stick them in the dark hull after what they just escaped, but she could not have them on the deck. There was not space without tripping over them, and they would be in the way if the crew had to fight. She did not know what to do with them.

Three women saved her the trouble. They were similar in looks and stature making it clear they were sisters. The one to the left spoke first.

"I can imagine you're wondering what to do with us now. Our father was a fisherman. We have no brothers, so we grew up sailing with him. We know how to navigate and captain a boat. Let us take the one docked below the cliff, and we will sail back to the Trondelag. We have enough women to manage even if most are inexperienced." She looked over at the group and tried not to show her own doubts. "It will be hard, but it is our best chance. We can't go to Scotland, and we have no home to return to. But if we can make it back to the Trondelag, then we have a chance to survive. None of us were thralls before this. We were free women. When Hakin left to kidnap the seer, Inga knew her brother would come. She gathered us and told us she would take us to safety. Instead, she brought us here. She gave us to the men with no thought to our ages or whether we're wed. If Hakin is recruiting that many men, then those of us wed are now widows. We have rights now, and we will each find a way to survive."

Erik looked to Freya who nodded. The three women wasted no time scuttling the others down the rock face and onto the waiting longboat.

"Do you think they'll make it?" Erik watched as the last one disappeared down the path.

"I haven't a clue. I don't doubt they can sail. However, I'm not convinced they won't encounter Hakin's pirates, and I'm not convinced they'll find anywhere accepting once they are home. But I wish them the best." Freya shrugged.

Her icy tone showed her guard was back up. Even after the confessions made only hours earlier, Freya was not ready to share all her true emotions. It would take more than a few emotional conversations and heated trysts to dismantle the defenses she spent a lifetime creating. Erik watched her before nodding. He knew prudence would be to keep his mouth shut, but he had not endured two months of the cold shoulder and then the emotional highs and lows of this trip to keep taking steps backwards. He stepped up to her and took her hand and gave it a brief squeeze before releasing it.

"It's all right to care. I do."

Freya's hackles went up. Her lips tightened into a thin line, and anger surged from her heart to every inch of her.

"About which one?"

Erik stared at her blankly before understanding her question.

"That was not what I meant. I can care for the wellbeing of others without caring about them individually. What I care most about is you not going back to shutting me out. Shut out the rest of the world, but never me. I will always be on your side. If nothing else, I want you to feel I am a safe harbor for all the things you believe you can't share with the rest of the world. I love you, Freya, and that's what it is to be loved."

"You wouldn't think me weak? To feel for them?"

"What weakness is there in that? You are the daughter of a jarl and soon to be the wife of a future jarl. If nothing else, it is your duty to care for others' wellbeing. I know you know that."

"That's different. They are our people. These women are not. They are the spoils of war."

Erik felt a weight he had not realized pressed on him fall away when Freya said "our." He was unaware that such a simple word would give him such a sense of relief.

"You're not even listening anymore. See." Freya tried to turn away.

"You think of them as 'our' people. You really are serious about marrying me."

Freya looked at him as if he was a simpleton.

"I said I would. Has something made you think I wouldn't? Why are you asking? This isn't what we were talking about." Freya crossed her arms.

"I am listening. Yes, those women should be ours to take home as thralls, but you can still appreciate their plight as a fellow person, or in your case as a fellow woman. It isn't a weakness. And if you still doubt that, remember the practicality. It wasn't mercy, it was practical. We can't fit them on the boat and keep them while we continue to scout. We haven't the food or the men to guard them. As for marrying me, I wasn't sure if you might come to your senses now that your ardor has cooled."

If another woman heard Erik use such a detached tone, she might have questioned his feelings, but it was what Freya needed. He understood her nature, and he knew what would soothe her. It was not dulcet tones filled with milk and honey. It was pragmatism. And Freya no longer cared who saw them. She stepped into his embrace.

"Practically speaking, we need to hurry. We shouldn't stand here discussing feelings. We are wasting time. But since we are, never wonder if my ardor has cooled because it hasn't. There isn't a moment of the day when I don't want you. And as for marrying you, we've given our word to one another. Don't think you can take it back without walking away a gelding. That's assuming I even let you walk. I have every intention of marrying you. I've wasted two moons we could have spent together. I'm not wasting any more time."

"They weren't wasted. Chasing you has been my greatest quest and made me fall even more madly in love with you. You are a maddening woman after all." He pinched her backside.

Freya was not to be outdone. She reached between then and wrapped her hand around the long, thick length that pressed against the front of his pants. She stroked him twice before dancing away.

"I have every intention of continuing to drive you mad."

She skipped away and darted down the path to their own waiting longboat. Once on the beach, Erik lifted her around the waist and flipped her up onto his shoulder. He knew he was taking a risk with her temper, but when she laughed, he knew he had not erred in his humor. He waded to the boat and up the gangplank with her still over his shoulder. Once on deck, he dropped her back onto her feet.

"Your captain has arrived. We shall sail."

The others stared for a moment before gales of laughter reached Freya's ears. She looked around and spotted Helga and Alva. Helga's expression was smug, but Alva's was warm. Perhaps Freya could make at least one more female friend.

"About damn time," one of Erik's men playfully griped.

Freya watched as coins exchanged hands.

"You bet on us?"

"Aye, captain. Whether the two of you would admit you wanted each other before the end of the trip or after."

"You assumed we would?"

"It was inevitable," chimed in a high-pitched voice from the crow's nest. Freund leaned over and called down. "I'll have my coin when I come down. Don't any of you forget what's mine."

Freya shook her head as she looked over at Erik. He was as surprised as she, so Freya knew he was not a part of the betting. She let them sort out their lots before issuing orders to get them underway. She set a course for the mainland.

"I think we should go to my mother's clan first. They may have information they can share. If nothing else, they may help us scout. They know the land, and they know the people." Erik came to stand beside Freya at the helm.

"I was thinking the same. I know you wore their plaid, but I wasn't sure if you were still close to her people."

"It took a while from what I understand. After the raid that killed my grandparents and uncle, my mother insisted my father shouldn't take her home again. She feared her clan wouldn't accept her for leaving with the enemy and would retaliate before they even made it off the boat. The story we spun wasn't far from what happened though. When my parents learned my mother was to have me, my father insisted that we go to see her clan. He saw the wisdom in his son knowing both sides of his family if he was to lead his people one day. He also regretted taking my mother away because she had a hard time being accepted at first." Erik shook his head before smiling wistfully. "I overheard them once when I was a child. Someone said something hurtful to my mother, but it upset my father more. I remember him saying he wished he had stayed in Scotland with her rather than bringing her back with him. She told him he was ridiculous, and that they were home. My father said he would have rather been the one to be unaccepted than to see the hurt people caused my mother. Anyway, we returned over the years, and my mother's people accepted their marriage. The Mackays haven't faced any raids since the one that brought my parents together. Everyone knows to attack the Mackays is to attack Rangvald, and except for this idiot Hakin, no one has wanted to take on my father or his allies. They will welcome us and help. I'm sure of it."

CHAPTER NINE

They sailed through the night and into the morning before Erik pointed out a castle that sat on an outcropping of rocks. There was a sandy beach below that would allow them to come ashore. They heard the alarm bells before they saw the men move on the battlements. Erik already instructed the crew not to draw their weapons and to wade ashore with their hands visible. Erik did not doubt they would be welcome, but his family had to recognize him first. As they made their way to the beach, he positioned himself in front of Freya. He shot her a quelling glance, and for once, she only nodded. Once on firm ground, Erik called up to the guards.

"I am Erik Rangvaldson, son of Rangvald and Lorna Mackay. We come with news and request the honor of your Highland hospitality."

"Cousin," Freya looked up to see a handsome dark-haired man close in age to Erik leaning over the wall walk. "Come up. You and your crew."

"That is Alexander. He is the son of my mother's cousin and now laird."

"That's how the name came to you."

"It is."

They entered the bailey to stares and murmurs. Freya looked around and felt keenly out of place. She was taller than any of the women she saw and rivaled even some of the men in height. The women all wore long tunics she knew they called kirtles. Her leather breeches made her stand out in yet another way. While she considered the Norse to be a cleaner people than the Scots, she felt filthy after days at sea and being caught in the rain. She wanted to smooth her hair back, but she would not give in to her self-consciousness. Most of the women were riveted on Erik, and she felt the sense of rivalry course through her. A need to wrap herself around his arm and claim him made her feel ill. She chided herself for the weakness. So instead she forced herself to stand with her shoulders back and chin held high.

"Cousin," Alexander greeted Erik by gripping his forearm and then pulling him into an embrace. They clapped each other on the back and laughed. "What brings you and your crew here?"

Alexander took in Freya's form and appreciation shone as his attention shifted to her.

"Who is your crew?"

"They are not my crew, Cousin. This is Freya Ivarsdóttir, and she is the captain of this expedition. They are her crew."

Erik uttered the last words as his hands itched to knock the smug look of interest from his cousin's face. The moment Alex beamed a smile at Freya, Erik regretted not introducing her first as his betrothed and then as the captain.

"Welcome, Lady Freya. If you are captain of this crew, you must undoubtedly be a fine sailor but also the daughter of a jarl. Or that would be my guess." Alex again smiled.

"I am." Alex's smiled faded at her succinct response, but it was back in place as he ushered them into the Great Hall. He called out orders for someone to make chambers ready for Erik, Freya, and the two married couples, along with space made in the barracks for the unwed warriors.

Freya looked to Erik as Alex stated the number of chambers. She was waiting for Erik to say something about them being betrothed, and she wondered if he considered sharing her chamber. They had sailed through the night and each warrior had to row since there was no wind. But Freya thought she and Erik would have shared her cabin if they had retired. Despite trying to catch his attention, Erik seemed oblivious until he glanced at her as they approached the stairs. His expression warned her to stay quiet.

Alex showed Erik to his chamber first, but Erik turned to follow them when Alex took Freya's elbow to lead her to her door.

"Don't fear, Erik. She won't get lost. The keep isn't that large."

Erik ground his teeth together.

"That may be, but I would still see Freya to her chamber. We have much to discuss about our plans now we have come ashore."

Alex looked like he would say more, but he continued walking. When they arrived at Freya's chamber, the two men squared off.

"Be out with it, Erik. Is she your woman?"

Freya growled softly.

"Freya and I are to marry. She accepted my offer, and I couldn't be happier." Erik stepped around to take Freya's hand before grinning at her. "I am as much hers as she is mine. And be careful, Alex. She is rather protective."

Freya glared at them both.

"I know you're standing right here, and we're being rude. I'm sorry." Alex and Freya looked at Erik as though he sprouted a second head, but he continued to smile. "We were, Alex."

Alex gave them a long look before excusing himself. Erik opened the door and ushered Freya in before closing it behind them. He turned the key and dropped the bar into place. Erik was on Freya a moment later. He gripped her bottom and lifted her, so she could wrap her legs around his waist. He walked them straight to the bed where he sat with her still straddling him.

"They have different notions about coupling than we do. Plenty of men bed women they are not married to, and there are many seven and eight moon babies born, but they are not open about it. They would not understand if I requested we share a chamber but admitted we aren't wed yet."

"Is that why you thought I was looking to you? I never expected to share a chamber with you. I looked at you because I wanted to know if I'll be expected to where one of those kirtles." Freya grinned. Whether they would share a chamber was what she wondered, and even though her body craved the time when they could finally come together, she was not sure she was ready for it to be now. When the fervor of passion abated, and her reasonable mind was in control, she was much slower to welcome Erik into her chamber or go to his.

Erik returned her grinned not fooled in the least.

"I told you. I'm in no rush. It doesn't have to be right this minute. It's best if it isn't since I'm sure a maid will bring a bath to you, but I needed to touch you."

"I needed it too," she leaned in for a quick kiss. "I feel like I have to make up for so much wasted time."

"None of it was wasted. It's what gave us the time to fall in love."

Freya shook her head.

"I think I've been in love with you all along."

Freya lowered her mouth back to his as they explored one another and what they could reach through clothes. Freya slid her hands into the neck of Erik's tunic, luxuriating in the smooth skin of his chest and shoulders. She reveled as she felt his muscles flexing as his hands squeezed her backside. She rocked her hips against him searching for the same friction that brought her to release in her cabin. Freya slid lips along the stubble to his ear. She flicked his lobe and sucked as she nipped at it.

"I love you, Erik," she breathed into his ear. He had never heard sweeter words than Freya admitting to her feelings. If he never heard another word, hearing her admission gave his battle-hardened heart peace.

"I love you, Freya. I have since the moment I saw you, and I will until my last breath. I pray I go first because I can't imagine living again without you."

Freya leaned back and cupped his face.

"Don't ever say something so horrible again. You think I could live without you? I don't want to go another day if we don't go together when we greet All Father."

Erik pulled her in for another searing kiss. He laid back, and Freya stretched across him.

"I thought you said we didn't have that much time," Freya trailed a finger along his collar bone fascinated by the line formed from where his tunic covered his skin from the sun.

"I shall make time."

A knock came at the door, and Erik groaned. He did not move, but Freya scrambled off him. Shaking his head, Erik went to open the door. A pretty, little brunette stood with towels draped over her arm, and there was a small army behind her with buckets and a tub.

"The laird sent me to assist with yer bath, ma laird." The woman purred as she took in the full length of Erik, and her eyes rested on his visible arousal. Erik wished he could cover himself. "Or assist with whatever else you might need."

Freya stepped into sight.

"That won't be necessary," Erik said before the woman could enter the chamber or Freya could scratch her eyes out. "I have the help I want."

The brunette raised an eyebrow as she surveyed Freya. Her opinion showed that she found Freya lacking. Erik was ready to shut the door in the impertinent servant's face. If he did not need the tub and buckets waiting in the hall, he would have.

"My laird, yer bath is ready for ye in yer chamber," the young woman was not deterred. She did not take her eyes off Erik and even went so far as to wink.

"In that case, if there is a bath already in my chamber, there is no need to set one up here. We shall make use of that one."

Erik turned and reached his hand out to Freya. She grabbed the sack that held her last set of clean clothes. She stepped forward towering over the servant. Freya did nothing to hide her gloating. On the way out, she threw over her shoulder, "I caused the problem, so I'll be the one to solve it."

Erik and Freya walked to his chamber and found a steaming bath sitting before the fire. Freya looked around the chamber and saw it was like the one they had given her. There was a massive four poster bed in the center with a table on each side. She noticed the two chairs someone moved to make room for the tub. It was a chamber to rival her own at home, but it was impersonal since it lacked the personal touches that her plunder lent her own chamber. She walked into the room, but when Erik did not follow her, she looked back to him.

"I didn't want to assume you would be all right with me seeing you bathe."

"I don't want you waiting in the passageway where that little strumpet can try to lay claim to you again."

"Envious?"

"Yes."

Erik smiled and walked into the chamber. Freya grasped the front of his tunic before she stretched to kiss him.

"Now you know how I felt watching Alex flirt with you. You just didn't do anything to stop him."

"You spoke about me as though I wasn't even there."

"True enough. But you are very much here now. Would you like me to wait behind the screen?" he pointed to a folded wooden partition. "Or would you like me to move it to shield the tub?"

"Neither." Freya unclasped and pushed the fur cape from Erik's shoulders then tugged at his tunic. "There is no point in trying to be discreet. We ruined that the moment the servants saw you in my chamber, and we confirmed it by coming here. We may as well enjoy our disgrace."

Erik lifted his shirt over his head as Freya stripped off her vest and tunic. They both stood there with only their boots and leather pants on.

"You should get in the tub before the water cools," Erik did not recognize the raspiness in his own voice.

Freya pulled off her boots and slid the breeches from her hips until they pooled around her feet. Erik thought he would collapse, his heartbeat was so rapid. He pulled his own boots off but kept his pants on.

"Get in, and I shall help you."

Freya shook her head.

"They at least have proper size tubs here. We shall both fit."

They looked at the tub. It was not that large. It would only fit them both if Freya lay on top of Erik.

"Freya, what I said the last time we nearly made love still holds true. There is no going back. I know you've agreed to marry me, but we never talked about how soon that might be. We are as good as wed the first time we couple. I will never let another man consider you available. I pledge all I am and all I have to you as I worship your body. I will be your husband as much as you are my wife."

"I would have it no other way. There is no one else for me, Erik. There never has been, and there will be no one else. I bind my soul to yours. The gods brought us together. They were a part of this just as much as they were when they brought Leif and Sigrid together. In fact, I'm sure Sigrid has known all along but let us come to this realization on our own. I want to be your wife as much as I want you to be my husband. I pledge all I am and all I have to you as I worship your body."

Freya helped ease the breeches off Erik. She stood in awe as she saw his rod for the first time. The night in the farmer's cottage had allowed her to touch it with no barriers, but to see it was another thing entirely. Even though she had limited experience, she was a shieldmaiden who traveled with men. She had seen her fair share and then some, but Erik's was the most impressive she had ever seen. Or perhaps it seemed that way because they would finally join. Erik scooped her into his arms as she squealed.

"I would hear you laugh every day."

"I do laugh every day. At you."

Erik nipped at her neck.

"I would have you laugh *with* me every day."

"I would like that."

Erik settled them into the bath with Freya draped along his chest. It only took a moment before they both shivered then laughed.

"We can't stay in this long before it's freezing."

"We're Norse, Erik. We dip in freezing water every time we bathe."

"Yes, after being sufficiently warmed by a hot water soak. We don't soak in the ice water."

"Afraid I won't be able to find them if you stay in here too long."

Erik growled as he reached for the soap and a linen.

"It shouldn't be hard since they'll be bright blue. How many more times can we be interrupted?"

"I don't suppose we'll know until we make love and can count back." Freya said tongue in cheek.

Erik flicked water at her, and Freya fought to swallow her screech, but it came out as more of a snort. They both dissolved into laughter as they rushed to bathe themselves.

"This is far too practical. It's not at all the leisurely soak I imagined." Erik griped with a smile. He stepped out of the tub to grab a drying linen. "Lay back. I will help you wash your hair."

Freya shot him a questioning look but did as he said. She popped back out of the water as Erik tucked the fabric around his waist. Freya pouted as Erik chucked her chin. He lathered up the soap and set to work. Freya had never felt anything so decadent and luxurious. Erik's fingers were strong, but his touch was gentle. He scrubbed her head, but it felt like a massage. Freya rested her head back until a thought dawned on her. She jerked up, but before she could lob accusations at him, he was prepared.

"I have never done this for a woman before, but I have sisters who were once little girls. Sometimes when we traveled, they needed help. I'm ten winters older than my oldest sister."

Freya settled back, but it was not the same. She felt restless now that he piqued her suspicions. She also marveled at how he always knew what she was thinking.

"Freya, I know about your past. I think I need to tell you about mine. I don't want you to hear it from anyone else." Erik paused until she nodded her head. He dreaded this because he knew he would ruin their happy moment together, but he could not wait any longer. "I have been with a handful of women. The demure type always attracted me, but I realized after meeting you, it was because I didn't want to deal with any of them making demands on me." Erik drew a deep breath as dread wound a noose around his heart. "Freya, I had a concubine for over a year."

Freya lurched forward and spun around.

"Wait, Freya. Listen. I ended things with her before I went on the last fishing voyage. At first, she didn't ask for anything and accepted things on my terms. I sought her out when I wanted, but towards the end it was rarely at all. She hinted that she wanted more. I had no interest in that, so I avoided her until I finally was fed up and ended things. She led me to believe she was fine with it, but when I returned from the fishing trip, I learned she spread rumors about my intentions to make her my official companion. I didn't have time to deal with it before going after Sigrid. Then I honestly forgot about her when you were there. There was a battle, and there was you. I didn't think about her until the maid flirted with me. I don't want you to arrive at your new home and hear half-truths or lies."

Freya dashed tears from her eyes. She knew she was being irrational getting upset over something that ended before Erik even met her, but she did not like the idea of him being in a relationship with someone else. It felt horrible even if it was inexplicable.

"Freya, talk to me," Erik's hushed tones were strained. Freya looked at him and saw anguish in his eyes.

"You really are worried because I'm upset. Are you worried I will call it off? Are you worried I will make a fuss when you take another concubine?"

The look of anguish morphed before her eyes. Anguish became anger.

"I never said I would take another concubine. Do you think I have so little honor? I pledged myself to you only moments ago, and you think I'm already planning to bed another woman. Do you even know me?"

Erik thrust the pitcher of clean water into her hands and rose to his feet.

"Wait, Erik. It's your turn to listen." Freya dumped the water over her head and rinsed the soap from it. She rose, and Erik stopped to watch her. She was still the most magnificent sight he had ever seen. "I know my father has never strayed, and I am sure your father never has either. But you are your own man. I would be a fool to assume you will be exactly as your father was. We never talked about it. I don't know what you expect from our marriage. You wouldn't be the first man to have a wife and keep a concubine. Some men keep multiple women. How can I know if I don't ask? I didn't think to ask until you brought it up."

Erik walked back to Freya and helped her step out of the bath. He wrapped a drying cloth around her.

"Fair enough. Freya, there will never be another. If I must spend every day for the rest of our lives telling you that, then so be it, but I wish you would believe me."

"I do. I just don't enjoy knowing that some woman held your attention for so long. Far longer than I've known you. There are women who know your body in a way I haven't yet learned, but there is a woman out there who knows you better than me. She must after a year with you."

"No. Not at all. I went to her when I wanted release. Nothing more. We didn't talk. She wasn't a confidante or even a friend. She was just a convenience. I know that makes me sound horrible, but it didn't seem so terrible. I never spent the entire night, or even more than five or ten minutes after we finished."

"I suppose it's not that much worse than my own experiences. The length of the time made my belly churn. I figured she must have gotten to know you well then."

"You know me better in two months than anyone else. You know me better than even my brothers and sisters or my parents."

"I suppose we shall deal with the rumors when we return."

"I warned her before I sailed to your homestead that she retracts what she'd said, or she would find herself banished. I will not tolerate her besmirching my honor. Then I didn't see her during our brief stop."

"Thank you for telling me. It's not what I wanted to hear, but you are right. I would have been furious to arrive at my new home to hear some story that wasn't the entire truth."

"So, we are all right?" Erik looked tentative, and Freya could not help smiling.

"It shall take far more than that to be rid of me."

"I'll never be rid of you any more than you can be of me."

They hurried to dress and made their way to the Great Hall. They gathered many looks, and Freya knew that her unusual clothing, along with her build, drew quite a few of them. But she also knew the whispers were from the gossip already spreading about her going to Erik's chamber as a maiden. Erik saw what Freya did. He slid the back of his hand along hers and when she did not pull away, he twined their fingers together. They stepped onto the dais just in time for the evening meal. The couple had been sequestered longer than they realized, having arrived just after the midday meal.

"Glad you could make it, Cousin," Alex smirked. "I wouldn't want you to starve your bonny bride-to-be."

Erik ignored Alex's teasing, but he was not pleased to hear Freya's laugh. He did not like his cousin amusing his intended. He knew it was unreasonable, but the thought grated on his nerves.

"Not to fear, laird, there was plenty to nibble on."

Erik coughed and Alex spluttered the wine he had just sipped. Both men stared at her. She raised her eyebrows and sat down between them.

"Erik, you have indeed found your match. You are a blessed man for sure."

CHAPTER TEN

The next three days passed like a winter storm blowing over the Highlands. The dark clouds of Erik's mood thickened until they could no longer hold the torrent that filled them. Alex, Freya, and Erik agreed that sending some of Alex's men to scout would be far more efficient since they knew the land and would not look out of place. Freya, Erik, and their crew trained alongside Alex and his warriors, and Erik did not need to feign his pride or admiration for Freya's ability to knock one warrior after another onto his arse. But he struggled to contain his anger as he watched the men line up to spar with Freya. It was not the fighting that bothered him. It was watching the men bumped into her as they fought, making it look like an accident when Erik was sure it was anything but, or when they extended a hand for help up only to make Freya lean forward so they could try to catch a glimpse down her tunic.

Accustomed to training with men who knew her from childhood and recognized she was the daughter of their jarl and sister to their future jarl, the men of Freya's tribe were wiser or at least less obvious in their attentions. Freya seemed immune to any attempts at charm and oblivious to their interest. Every time they called for a rest, Freya came to Erik's side if he was not already there waiting for her. Erik wanted to bash in the faces of the men who trailed after her.

"Cousin, ye could kill with the look on yer face. Have ye turned into a silent berserker?"

Erik turned to look at his smirking cousin who stood next to him as they looked out on the field of warriors. Despite their difference in coloring, they resembled each other and their personalities were similar. They got on well as children and liked each other as adults, but Erik was not in the mood for his cousin's taunting.

"I never took ye for the possessive type."

"I never had a reason to be in the past."

"Ye ken the lass only has eyes for ye. I dinna understand why, but she does."

"And every man in your clan who can see has eyes for her."

"But whose bed is she warming?"

Erik ground his teeth. Alex hit on the real reason for Erik's frustration. Freya was not warming anyone's bed but her own. The gossip flew about the keep before the end of the first evening meal. While Freya did not have many female friends, she was sensitive to the opinion held by other women. The condescending looks thrown her way from the women were enough to cool her ardor. She understood by the end of the meal what Erik meant when he said the Highlanders had different ideas about sex than the Norse. She did not want to spend the time they had there being judged as a whore. Freya kissed Erik goodnight each night and dropped the bar to her door. Erik returned to his chamber alone with little consolation other than his hand.

"No one's."

Alex spun around to look at Erik.

"What?"

"Your women made their opinions clear once they heard Freya accompanied me back to my chamber to bathe. Before the first evening was through, Freya wasn't interested in ruining her reputation any further. We both sleep alone."

"I had nay idea. She doesnae even let ye sneak in?"

"No."

"Nay wonder ye're fit to be tied. Why nae find one of the serving lasses who's willing to ease yer suffering?"

Erik thought his head would explode. Anger thrummed through him as he balled his fists. He would not strike his family member nor a laird in front of his people. But the temptation was almost more than he could withstand. Alex watched as his cousin transformed into the berserker he mentioned earlier. Alex held up his hands in surrender.

"I didna mean any harm. I didna realize yer feelings ran that deep." Alex waited for Erik to calm, and it took so long for Erik to unclench his fists and his jaw, Alex was not sure he would. Once Erik regained his composure, Alex prodded again. "If ye love her that much, why are ye letting these men chase her? Stake yer claim once and for all. It would drive me barmy to watch ma woman with all these men. I dinna ken how ye do it."

"I do it because Freya is a warrior the same as we are. She needs to train just as much as any of us. She can't just spar against only me or even our crew. If we are to fight in the Highlands, we would all do well to learn more of how you fight."

"Aye, so ye can raid us with more ease," Alex's grin took the sting from his words.

"If the clans could stop fighting one another, they might have the energy to fight us. It's not our fault Highlanders can't keep up. Besides that, I promised I wouldn't stake a claim and take her choices away."

The men grinned at one another, and Erik felt himself relax for one of the few times over the past three days. However, it was short lived as a crowd converged around Freya and the largest warrior Alex had. Erik tensed as he watched the man's broadsword sweep down towards Freya. She was far stronger than any woman Erik ever saw, but the man was colossal. He would have posed a challenge even for Erik, given the momentum his enormous build gave him. Erik stepped forward, but Alex blocked him. Erik watched in horror as Freya allowed the blade to come within an inch of her shoulder before she spun and pressed a knife against the man's ribs.

"Do you relent?" she asked.

The man roared, and Freya jumped out of his way. The ensuing sword fight created a cacophony as their weapons ground against each other and the fighters grunted with effort. Freya's arms burned as she blocked one thrust or parry after another. Freya patiently held her own, having sized up her opponent before they began. He was used to taking advantage of his size, which lent force to his swings. He was agile for being a head taller and at least ten stone heavier than Freya, who banked on her endurance being stronger than his. She had spent her entire life fighting twice as many warriors as her male counterparts during every training session just to prove herself. She was her harshest judge, so she pushed beyond reasonable boundaries time and time again. Freya prayed it paid off now. She watched the sweat dripped from the man's brow just as it did from hers. She danced around him, blocking one sweep of his blade after another. He tried using his height to his advantage, but every time he raised his arm high enough, Freya thrust forward with her knife, forcing him to jump back. Tiring, the man lobbed insults hoping to distract her.

"I'm surprised ye have enough fight left in ye after spending all night rolling around with that heathen lover of yers."

Freya said nothing.

"Cat got yer tongue? Or ye too out of breath to speak? Need to conserve the little energy ye have left?"

"The hot air coming from you is stifling."

Freya garnered a few chuckles which led her opponent to swear before lunging forward once more.

"Are ye this much of a hellion in bed? Perhaps we should put these swords aside and ye can use a real one."

"When you find one, let me know. Till then, I like the ones I have."

More men laughed, but Erik did not see the humor in watching Freya have to defend herself and her reputation. He knew they should have been more circumspect, and the consequences of their indiscretion were the taunts along with the other men's leers.

"So ye are the Norseman's whore."

With one word, the entire mood shifted. The crowd became tense as they waited to see Freya's reaction. When she gave none, their eyes flicked back and forth between the opponents and the tension escalated as they feared, rather than marveled, her silent strength. Erik had heard and seen all he could tolerate. He pushed past his cousin, and Alex let him. Both Freya and Erik's honor were being called into question. Erik pushed his way to the front of the crowd but once there, he did not move. He would do nothing to distract Freya. The fight ended only a moment later. Fed up with the taunts and wasted energy, Freya struck out in a series of moves no one expected. She thrust her sword upwards with the flat of her blade contacting his and pushed with all the strength she could muster in that arm. It gave her an opening to sweep her leg out. She made contact first with his ankle and then the back of his knee. As his knee crumpled, she dropped her knife and threw all the force she had into her other arm as her fist contacted his nose. Blood spewed forth, splattering her and the ground. Just before he sank all the way to the ground, she jerked her knee into his groin. On the ground now with one hand cupping his cods and the other his nose, the man moaned as Freya's booted foot kicked his chest and he rolled onto his back. Her foot hovered over his throat.

"Relent?"

"Aye," the ogre spluttered.

No one moved. No one said a word. It seemed as if no one dared to breathe. Freya looked unmussed and unruffled. Sweat clung to her brow and a few hairs stuck to her forehead, but otherwise, no one who had not seen the battle would have known she spent the past quarter hour defending herself against a beast of a man. Freya scooped up her knife and looked around. When her eyes landed on Erik, she beamed and stepped towards him.

Freya saw emotions in Erik's eyes she never saw before. It scared her enough she was not sure he would welcome her. She had few choices though. She had already turned her attention to him and moved in his direction. Freya could not alter her course now without making it obvious. Her eyes darted about, and she knew everyone was just as enraptured with what would happen next as they were with the fight she just won.

Erik saw the moment Freya hesitated. He saw doubt and fear where there had been none only a second ago. He wanted to kick himself. He directed his feelings of anger at all the men he was sure goaded her into that fight, to the man who insulted her and endangered her with a fight that went beyond training, to his cousin for not reeling his men in sooner, and to himself for being stuck with no choice but to watch. He respected Freya too much to dishonor and humiliate her by intervening, and so he was forced to watch the only woman he ever loved fight a man who dwarfed even him. He moved towards Freya and saw the fear drop from her eyes. She had not feared his anger but his rejection. Erik wanted to kick himself all over again.

They stood before one another acutely aware they were still the center of attention. As warriors, there was little to be done. As lovers, both wanted to fall into the other's arms. Only the former was an option if they were to avoid confirming the accusations lobbed at Freya.

"Go to the cottage," Alex whispered.

Erik shot him a glance of appreciation. He forgot about the cottage Alex's parents had maintained. It was the home Alex's mother grew up in, but it was a refuge for the couple when they wanted time alone away from the keep. It sat near the loch and was private, while still enjoying the safety provided by the castle. Erik tilted his head in the loch's direction, and Freya nodded. She smiled at Alex before following Erik.

Once they were out of the lists, but even though they knew others could see them, they joined hands.

"Are you angry with me?"

"Not at all. I am furious with that beast for insulting you and taking that fight far beyond anything meant for training. But I'm proud of you."

"You didn't seem like it."

"Freya, what was I supposed to do other than watch you fight a man who had every intention of not only humiliating you but hurting you? He wanted more than anything to win. He wanted to prove you inferior as a woman and a shieldmaiden. And he would bed you right now just to prove himself still a man. Then he would share the details with everyone who would listen. You know I would never intervene, at least not until there was no other option to save your life. You are a warrior, and I've known that all along. The only difference is this time I couldn't fight back to back with you. I just had to watch."

Freya stopped and pulled Erik to look at her. She had already wiped the blood from her face but passed her sleeve over her mouth once more before cupping his face and stretching onto her toes.

"I love you, Erik Rangvaldson. I love you with a ferocity I can't contain, and I don't want to any longer. I don't give a shite what any of them say anymore. After that fight, there isn't a one of these Highlanders who will think I'm a lady, and I don't care. What I do care about is you. I am yours, and I will not hide it again. I could have spared us both this if my pride hadn't gotten in the way. I didn't want to be the object of gossip, but I swapped one evil for another. Now they will judge me for winning against their best warrior. If people are going to talk, then let them talk about that. They can let their tongue wagging keep them warm at night. I prefer having you keep me warm."

"What are you saying?" Erik whispered.

"I'm saying, I don't care about these prudish Highlanders or their beliefs about bedding one another before being wed. We are not Scots. Or at least I'm not. I don't have to live by their customs."

Erik pulled her tightly into his arms as he kissed her. They drank one another in as the past three days' tension fell away. The rustling of a bush with a rabbit that scampered out pulled them apart. They walked to the loch in silence but with their arms wrapped around each other's waist. When they walked past the cottage, Erik ran inside and found a lump of soap and drying linens. They found a secluded spot on the shore and stripped off their clothes before wading in. The water was icy but not unlike a fjord at home. Neither wasted time. They lathered themselves, and Freya took extra care to be sure she scrubbed the blood from her face and hair. Shivering, they gathered their clothes and raced back to the cottage. It did not take long before Erik had a blaze in the hearth, and Freya found a jug of mead and two mugs. They warmed themselves until Erik no longer saw gooseflesh on Freya's arms. He took their mugs and placed them on the table before laying his linen over the stool to dry.

Freya could not believe her eyes. She saw Erik's body the first day at the keep when they bathed together. She even saw it only minutes before when they bathed at the loch. But the way the firelight glowed across his skin mesmerized her. His skin glowed as his muscles tautened and relaxed with each of his movements. Freya pulled her linen from her body and spread it over the other stool. Erik's cock jerked as he took in the stunning beauty of Freya standing bare in front of him.

Now I understand the reaction women have when they stare at me. How is it I've never lacked confidence before, but one vinegar-tongued shrew brings me to my knees? Who am I fooling? It's because I've never felt anything was at stake. Now everything worth having is at stake.

Erik's lips twitched, and Freya raised an eyebrow. He shook his head, but that did not deter her.

"You've thought of something that made you smile. What was it?"

"Nothing. I was enjoying the view."

Freya's curiosity demanded to know why he would not share his thoughts.

"That I don't believe." She crossed her arms and tilted her head to raise her chin in defiance.

"You'll think me an arse if I tell you."

"I already think that often enough. What would be different?" Freya smiled.

Erik shook his head. He was certain his confession would sour the moment, but he did not want withholding the truth to be the reason for their argument. He would rather Freya think him an arse than believe she could not trust him.

"I thought now I understand the reaction women have when they stare at me."

Erik watched the inevitable transformation. He saw the color rise in her neck and flood through her cheeks. Her eyes flashed. Her anger made her resemble a magnificent Valkyrie, but he knew he would not think it so magnificent when he was on the receiving end of her temper.

"Then find one of them to stare at." Freya turned towards the fire with her back straight, but Erik saw the slight rounding of her shoulders. He would rather see her angry than defeated.

Erik moved behind her and slid an arm around her waist as the other hand brushed her hair away. His fingers trailed along her collarbone.

"I didn't say *I* look at women that way. I warned you I would sound like an arse. I understand the looks of appreciation and desire now that I look upon you. I've never seen anything more beautiful than you. You've been this elusive dream since the moment I met you. I've gotten snippets during this trip, but now I can see this dream through." Erik dipped his head to kiss her shoulder. "Freya, I am in awe of everything about you. Your beauty is blinding, but you are so much more than that. You have a brilliant mind, a kind heart despite how you hide it, and you're braver than most of the men I know. You have a reckless streak that both terrifies and amuses me. I am a moth drawn to your flame, and I fear you shall burn me alive."

Freya listened as Erik spoke, and she felt herself lean back into his embrace.

"What could you fear?" she rasped, her voice huskier than usual.

"A great many things." Erik splayed his hand over her belly and the other slid from her collarbone down between her breasts. "I fear you shall tire of me. Freya, you can have your choice of any man in your tribe. You could have any man in the Trondelag, to be honest. Why choose me when there are many other worthy men?"

"I choose you because you're the only man who, try as you might to irritate me, makes me happy. I choose you because you are the only man I feel myself around. You take my temper in stride, you respect my choice to be a shieldmaiden, and I don't think you'll ever try to change me."

"I have no desire to ever change you. Who you are is who I love. I don't want any other woman. I don't want any other version of you. But can you say the same?"

Freya turned in his arms and rested her hands on Erik's heart. She looked into his eyes and saw his worry.

"Freya, you even have Scottish men trailing after you. There is no man who meets you and doesn't desire you. What happens when you meet someone you admire just as much?"

Freya's brow furrowed as she listened to Erik. She never suspected his insecurities ran as deeply as he showed them now. It surprised her that a man such as himself felt any doubt, let alone about a woman declaring her love.

"Erik, do you think I'm fickle?"

"No. But I know I'm not the only man who wants your attention, and I know there are many men who would make a strong match for you. What about when you meet someone else?"

"You worry about this, don't you?"

"How could I not? Look at how easily I fell in love with you. What happens when another man falls in love with you and wants you as much as I do?"

"Then he should have gotten to me sooner. Too bad for him because I am already taken. Erik, you ask me to believe you want no other woman. You've promised me you won't stray. Can you not trust me?"

"It's not that I believe you would be unfaithful. I trust your honor. I just worry you will choose someone else. You have every right to leave our marriage if you wanted to. What if you decide that's what you want? That you want someone more?"

Erik's voice was only hushed murmurs by the time he finished. Freya pushed the hair from his brow as she stared into his eyes.

"Erik, I've met many men in my life. Most are Norse but not all. Never have I ever considered any of them for my husband. I could have married several times over since I am old by most people's standards. I understand now why none of them interested me before. The gods hadn't led me to you yet. I love you, Erik. I love you even more for admitting how you feel rather than keeping it to yourself. It would have only made your doubt and fears fester, and it would have been what drives us apart rather than me finding anyone else. I never imagined you worried so much."

"And I hate admitting such weakness. I feel I sound like a nagging woman, but I fear this. You are so special. Who would not want you?"

"I can think of at least one," Freya grinned. "I wonder if his cods still hurt."

Erik smiled back, but Freya could tell he was unconvinced.

"Erik, I can keep telling you, promising you, that I will never want another, but at some point, you must trust me. Trust yourself and give yourself more credit. Don't you think I fear the same thing? You are the most handsome man I have ever met. I see women stare after you. I've told you as much. I hate it. I hate every single time I see another woman salivate. Every time I see one move in your direction. I especially hate how courteous and flirtatious you are. I feel resentment and rage unlike anything I've ever experienced before. But I also believe you when you say you haven't been with another woman since before you met me, and when I think over everything I have seen of you, I realize you're telling me the truth. There's no real proof to think otherwise. I choose you, and I choose to believe in you. I need you to do the same. Follow your own sound advice. You've already told me more than once. Believe in yourself. Believe in me. Believe in us." Freya cupped his jaw and brought his mouth so close their lips brushed as she spoke. "Believe because there is no other choice. I'll never let you go."

CHAPTER ELEVEN

Erik felt the doubt that plagued him since he first met Freya slip away. The covetousness and self-consciousness were new to him, and he had not known how to process them. They often rivaled his feelings for Freya, and he worried they would never subside. But her words of encouragement and reassurance were a balm to the ache that resided so deeply within Erik's mind.

"I admit I needed to hear that, Freya. I have no experience being in love, and the thought of losing you to anything, particularly another man, is an anguish I didn't know how to bear. Your words bring me relief I didn't understand how badly I needed."

"I never would have imagined you to be self-conscious. I still don't understand why you are, but I will do all I can to reassure you. I don't want anyone else, Erik. Being in love is new to me, too. Why do you think I fought it for so long? It terrified me you would be the one to leave."

"I've trailed after you for months with a singular focus. Did you think I would give up?"

"I thought maybe it was the pursuit you enjoyed."

"I may be a glutton for punishment when it comes to how I train, but it's been agony praying you would notice me."

"Oh, I noticed you. From the beginning. You threw me off kilter, and I didn't enjoy feeling out of control. Then I feared giving in, in case this was a game to you."

"I may have teased you, but this was never a game. I don't think you see just what value you hold or how remarkable you are. If you did, you would understand my fear."

"I think we share the same anxiousness. We echo one another. I never imagined my fears would be yours, too."

Erik lowered his mouth to hers. The time for talking was at an end. They both spoke their minds and their hearts. Now their bodies were ready to express the rest. Freya pressed her long, lean body against his and indulged in the feel of his broad shoulders encasing her as his arms held her pinned against his body. His cock throbbed between them, an outward reminder that none of their ardor cooled during their discussion. Erik cupped Freya's bottom and lifted her. She wrapped her legs around his waist and moaned as the tip of his rod prodded her entrance.

Freya remembered Erik's words from when they were on Orkney.

"There is no going back after this, Erik."

"I only want to move forward with you as my wife. I will make love to you and I will claim you as my wife. You are mine now, and there will be no doubt in anyone's mind, not ours and not someone else's, that you are my wife and my woman until we meet again in Valhalla." Erik pressed down on Freya's hips as his surged forward. He entered her with ease. Her channel was slick with its readiness for him. Freya clenched around his length and gave a satisfied moan as she shut her eyes.

"Good gods. I never imagined joining with you would feel this good. Believe me when I promise you I will never let you go. You are my man and my husband. Let anyone try to stand between us, and it will be my sword or my claws that keep them away."

They kissed, wild and rough, as Erik walked them to the bed tucked away in the corner. Freya clung to him as he crawled onto it and lowered her to the mattress. They lay still for a moment gazing at one another before need overshadowed everything else. The passion, born of love, physical need, and denial, drove them together. Erik knew he was being rough, but every time he tried to ease the force of his thrusts, Freya's nails bit into his backside and she gave a moan of frustration. She dug her heels into the bed as she lifted her hips in tandem with Erik's. Their give and take mirrored their banter, each giving and receiving what they needed. Freya's hands roamed over Erik's body as she felt her toes curl. She was insatiable for the feel of him on top of her and inside her. She wanted to know every inch of him, so he was no longer a mystery but something so familiar she could not remember a time before him. Erik growled and rolled them over.

"Not fair," he grumbled as he pressed her breasts to his face. He alternated suckling them as his hands caressed Freya's body. He had felt nothing like it. There was strength and power beneath the skin he knew tasted of honey. Her body was a marvel. No woman ever looked as feminine as Freya the few times he saw her in a gown, and yet there was no one fiercer than her on the battlefield. The toned muscles of her limbs and body gave way to the soft firm flesh of her breasts. His teeth tugged at her nipples until they became distended aching nibs that begged for more attention. She cupped them in offering as she sat back. Erik watched as she bounced with her head thrown back and her back arched. She looked like the goddess her parents had named her for, Freyja. But the need to feel connected drew their bodies together, and Freya leaned down to press chest-to-chest with Erik. His grip was almost painful as he filled his hands with the globes of her backside, but the intensity of their lovemaking only drove them higher until they both surrendered to the pleasure that surged through them. The aftershocks rippled through them as Erik continued to guide Freya's hips as she rocked against him, drawing out her pleasure through a second wave of spasms. When at last her body was drained and boneless, she lay limp across Erik's chest.

Erik held Freya as his eyes drifted closed while he struggled to fill his lungs with enough air. He worried he would suffocate her as he realized he was clinging to her rather than embracing. He loosened his grip but felt her shake her head. When he enfolded her in his arms again, he felt her deep contented sigh. They laid still so long they each wondered if the other fell asleep. The air cooled their glistening bodies, and soon the chill forced them to shimmy under the covers.

"I wish we could stay here forever, tucked away from everyone and everything."

"That might push the limits of your cousin's hospitality."

"True, but I'm not ready to share you with the rest of the world. I would stay nestled away here for a while."

"I like just being Erik and Freya rather than future jarl and daughter of a jarl. A break from the duties and responsibilities, even if for only a night, would be such a treat."

"I'm in no rush to return to the keep if you aren't."

"I'm not, and to be honest, I haven't slept well since we arrived. It's not the same as being in my chamber in my parents' longhouse where I have slept since I was a child or the same as sleeping in camp where I can find you. It's been unsettling to be alone in a strange place without having you near. I know I traveled for years before I met you, but nothing is the same as it used to be."

"I haven't slept well either. I don't enjoy knowing you're down the hall in a chamber anyone can find."

"You know I wouldn't open the door to any man but you. Not unless the keep were under attack or burning down around our ears."

"I trust you. I don't trust a damn one of those men."

Freya's stretched along his body and settled onto her side with an arm thrown over his chest and her leg entangled with his.

"I never thought the first night I spent with you would be one with much sleep."

"Maybe the morning after our first night, but I have no intention of letting you sleep tonight."

Erik rolled Freya onto her back and eased his way down the bed. Freya craned her neck to watch Erik's descent until his shoulders rested beneath her thighs. He nudged her legs over his shoulders as he blew cool air on her heated flesh. The contrast between his breath and the heat radiating from her made her quiver. This only stirred the ache that lingered low in her belly. Erik's fingertips brushed along the inside of her thighs, creeping towards her entrance but fluttering away before making contact. Freya tried to lift her hips off the mattress to meet his touch, but Erik nipped at her thigh, then licked the spot to soothe it. Freya's moan filled Erik's ears, and he knew he was treading a fine line between fun and frustration. He wanted to tease out the moment and heighten Freya's desire, but he did not want to ruin it by pushing her physical patience too far. Erik kissed a trail back up to her seam as he took in the honey scent of her skin. He flicked his tongue over and over as Freya's hips moved to meet him. She mewled as she felt the tension building inside her.

"Erik, please stop teasing me. I'll do whatever you want. I'll beg, but don't make me wait. I can't stand it. My body aches for you so much it hurts." Freya's voice cracked as she pleaded.

Erik watched her as he thrust his fingers into her. Unlike in the farmer's cottage, he did not hesitate. He entered her as he sucked her bud into his mouth. He applied pressure until her hips arched off the bed. He held her gaze until she could not keep her eyes open any longer. The sight of Freya coming apart again dazzled Erik as his mouth and fingers pleasured her. He pulled himself up over her and entered her with one swift push. Her arms and legs came around him and locked him against her. This time their motions were slow as they lavished each other with attention to the fine details, discovering what the other liked and wanted. As Erik felt the pressure build within his body and the telltale tingle began at the base of his spine, a thought niggled at the back of his mind.

"Freya, should I pull out?"

Freya's eyes sprung open.

"What?"

"I didn't ask you before, but I don't know if you're ready to have children yet. Marriage will change our lives enough, but I don't know if you want that change to include motherhood. Should I pull out?"

Freya stared at him as her mind tried to shift from pleasure to pragmatism. She knew what she wanted to say, but Erik's body joined with hers and the pleasure they gave each other was enough to make her change her mind. But her practical nature won. She appreciated Erik's consideration of what she might want for her future.

"I'm not ready to be a mother." Freya watched Erik and for a moment worried she disappointed him.

"Then we will be very careful until you are."

Freya cupped his jaw as she poured all her love and devotion into their kiss, and she felt Erik's seep into her soul. It was only another moment before spasms rocked through Freya's body, and Erik withdrew to spill across her belly.

It was not long after that they curled up and drifted to sleep in one another's arms. They spent the rest of the afternoon and well into the night dozing and making love until the early hours of the morning when they were both too exhausted to do anything but drop into a deep slumber.

The sun was well into the sky when Freya and Erik awoke to a pounding on the door. Erik covered Freya before grabbing his tunic and pulling it on. He opened the door just a crack and looked out. It was one of his warriors with news of the scouts. After receiving the news, Erik stalked back over to the bed. Freya watched as he waggled his eyebrows at her.

"Look what has turned up in my bed. I believe it is a *hulder* who has found her way inside this cottage."

"I am no woodland nymph. Perhaps you are a *nacken* sent to make me fall in love with you."

"You think I could be a *Fossegrim* who left my watery home to lure you."

"I'm not sure what you are," Freya giggled, "but you have lured me in."

Erik threw back the cover and crawled onto the bed as though he was a cat stalking its prey.

"Now you look more like a *wegie*," Freya laughed again.

"Maybe that is fitting. After all, the goddess Freyja has cats to pull her chariots. Perhaps I am a wild cat you found and are trying to tame."

Freya sat up and opened her arms to Erik.

"What if I don't want you tame?"

"Then you have nothing to worry about."

"And if I should want you to stay by my side, loyal just as the *wegie* is to Freyja?"

"I am already by your side."

Erik lifted Freya to straddle his lap as he kneeled on the bed. He stroked the hair off her shoulders and wrapped a lock around his finger. It was close to winter, so her hair had darkened to the color of thatch, but he was certain it would bleach white in summer. He was so lost in thought it was not until Freya pulled one of his locks of hair that he realized she had been speaking.

"I asked, what did your warrior want?"

"The scouts were spotted. They should be at the keep within the hour."

Freya scrambled off Erik's lap.

"We need to head back then."

"We have an hour."

Freya pursed her lips and shot him a withering look.

"Even if they weren't on their way back, the morning is gone. What will everyone think?"

"I thought you were done worrying about what others think about us. We aren't Scots. We're Norse."

"I'm not worried about that. I don't care anymore if they think me unchaste. What I care about is them thinking I'm lazy."

Erik laughed as he followed Freya over to their clothes. He watched her as she pulled her clothes back on. He shook his head ruefully. Getting dressed was the opposite of what Erik wanted to be doing with the woman he now considered his wife.

"Stop staring at my backside and hurry." Freya's voice was muffled as she pulled her tunic over her head.

"But it's such a fine one." Erik patted her, and she scouted away. "I can think of quite a few things I'd like to do to it and with it. Why don't I show you?"

"Tonight." Freya shot him a heated look that did nothing to cool the heat surging to his groin. "I need to return to the keep for fresh clothes anyway. These still have dirt and blood on them from yesterday."

Erik handed Freya her vest and cloak before fastening his.

"What shall it be? Do you move to the chamber I've been using, or do I move to the one you've used? We aren't sleeping apart anymore."

Freya laughed as she shook her head.

"I'll move to yours. I have less to pack," she gloated, dashing to the door as she strapped her sword across her back.

CHAPTER TWELVE

Freya and Erik dashed back to the keep but not before they looked back over their shoulder at the little cottage. As they approached the postern gate of the castle wall, Erik slowed them and took Freya's hand. He gave it gentle squeeze as he entwined their fingers.

"Do you consider yourself my wife yet?"

"Aren't I? I mean I know we haven't gone through the rituals, but we've made the pledge just like we would in front of everyone else."

"That's why I ask. If standing before our shaman and your family is what you need to feel married, then I understand."

"I want us to do those things when we return, but waiting for that doesn't make us any less married in my eyes. We're not much different than Leif and Sigrid, and I never thought less of their marriage."

"Then I can reintroduce you as my wife?"

"No," Freya grinned, "but you can reintroduce yourself as my husband."

"Gladly."

They stepped through the gate as riders entered beneath the portcullis. They hurried over to meet Alex as he came down the keep steps.

"Well rested, I see," Alex gloated. "You're welcome."

"Thank you, Cousin." Erik gave a tight-lipped response, and when Alex's smile fell, Erik laughed clapping him on the back. "Have you met my wife?"

Erik wrapped his arm around Freya, and she stepped into the shelter of his embrace. She felt shy even though she had fought and won against the largest man in the clan only the day before. Erik's voice carried and several heads turned towards them. The whispers began as did the jealous looks from the women and the leers from the men. If anyone had not heard they spent the night together in the cottage, they all would now.

"Ye're nae married. We havenae a priest here. She's just unchaste." A voice rose above the crowd and the responding buzz sounded like an angry swarm.

"Why would I need your priest? I'm Norse. But if you are wondering, we honored one of your traditions. We handfasted." Freya listened as Erik's voice hardened from the jovial tone only a moment ago. He looked about the crowd and dared anyone to speak against them again. Alex crossed his arms and stood shoulder to shoulder with his cousin.

"Having a new cousin is exciting. She's an improvement on the old one," Alex's words were humorous, but his tone brooked no argument. "I'm happy to call Freya family."

The whispers ended with those final words, and the scouts joined them on the steps. The group of seven moved inside and secluded themselves in Alex's solar. Alex pulled out maps and spread them across the large wooden table that took up the center of the chamber. Chairs sat around it for council meetings, and his desk was pushed back into a corner where he could work when there was no one else there. A fire already roared in the hearth, and it was a cozy room even if it was the place where they planned battles.

"What did ye find?" Alex asked one of his men, Keith.

"Quite a lot. We ken this Hakin has tried recruiting from several of the clans along the coast. We ran into a Gunn patrol that ran him off their land about a fortnight ago. Hakin tried to convince half their guardsmen to desert and join his mercenary army. He made the mistake of not learning who he was speaking to before he made promises. He didn't ken the laird is only eight and ten and was part of the group he addressed. Hakin tried to convince the men to desert right in front of their laird. They laughed him out of their bailey."

"Do you know where he is now?" Freya asked.

"The last anyone saw of him, he was camped where our land meets both the Sutherlands and MacLeods. We rode through Sutherland and learned that his brother, Grímr, is recovering in their camp. He's close to healed but bitter. There are rumbles that Grímr is recruiting for Hakin, too, but he's paying the men extra to align themselves with him and not Hakin."

"So what Sigrid saw was true. Grímr plans to outmaneuver his brother. He wants what Hakin has and is willing to let Hakin gain this army before taking it for himself. He lets Hakin pay for the men but sweetens the deal by adding a little extra. This way he gets what he wants but still keeps most of his money. If his wife is selling women as bed slaves and his brother is pirating, and he claims to be convalescing, then he gets his share while doing little work other than training and sparring." Freya deduced and looked around the table to see the agreement on the men's faces.

"So, the question becomes who do we go after first? We have orders not to engage, which is fine, but we still need more information. Do we find their camp and see what is going on for ourselves, or do we sail home to gather our armies? Do we wage a war against another Norseman here in Scotland? If we scout further and find Hakin and Grímr, are we prepared to fight?" Erik rattled off the same questions Freya was pondering.

"I think we have little choice but to scout more. We still don't know which clans on the mainland are supporting him. We don't know where Inga went. She wasn't on the farm, so is she with Hakin and Grímr?"

"Or do we return home and gather our boats and lay in wait at their cave for when they return for the bounty we've already claimed?"

"I don't think that'll be as successful. Only one of them will come for the gold, so even if we defeat that one, there will be another brother still left to fight," Freya pointed out. "I think we travel further inland using Mackay scouts, if you'll allow it Alex, and find their exact location. If we find their camp, then the Mackays should be able to tell us whose plaids we see. Then we return home for more warriors."

Freya paused as she looked at the Mackays in the room. She left the rest of her thoughts unsaid but they were clear. Once Freya and Erik's tribes returned to Scotland, it would be to raid whichever clan was helping Hakin. They would leave little left of that clan. She would not say the obvious. She did not want to put her new family in the middle where they must decide whether their loyalty lay with their fellow Highlanders or their distant Norse family.

"I will ride out with ye, and I'll bring two score men along with us," Alex interjected. "I would have Hakin and Grímr understand the Highlands arenae their hunting grounds for men. They want more warriors; they will need to find Norsemen willing to fight for them."

"Thank you, Alex. Then our goal is to find Hakin and Grímr and learn who they are hiring, but I want us to learn where my Aunt Inga is hiding. I need to tell my father the role his own sister plays in this. I don't believe she's innocent at all." Freya heard the regret in Erik's voice, and Alex clapped a hand on his shoulder.

"Ye canna pick yer family, but ye can pick yer allies. We are here for ye."

They spent the rest of the morning and into the afternoon pouring over the maps and devising strategies for numerous outcomes. While Freya garnered various stares during the evening meal, she recognized most were curiosity. She knew she stood out. A few harbored ill feelings towards her for both winning Erik and winning against their greatest warrior. She held her head with pride but focused her attention on those seated at the dais. Erik began the meal holding her hand under the table, but as he sensed more of the looks, he lifted their hands to rest in clear sight. Freya tensed, but he rubbed his thumb over her knuckles to reassure her. He made no other outward signs of affection, remembering Freya shied away from them even at home. He knew she was self-conscious about appearing emotional and weak in front of others. However, he was proud to sit beside her, and he wanted to let everyone know he was just as committed as she was. Neither was available.

When the evening meal ended, they moved before the large hearth for cups of warmed mead. Freya felt herself relax for the first time within the castle. Since arriving in Scotland, the only time she felt unguarded was the night before in the cottage. She felt herself growing tired and her lids heavy. Erik slid her closer to him on the bench they shared, and she did not fight him when he nudged her to rest against him.

If this is what it is to be in love, to be married, then I should have pulled Erik to the altar the moment I met him.

"I've been trying to convince you of that since I arrived." Erik whispered.

Freya startled awake realizing she spoke aloud.

"No one but me heard you. You mumbled it. I think it's time we retired. You can't keep your eyes open."

"I feel a bit off."

"Are you falling ill?"

"No, I'm never sick. This is different. I didn't drink that much, but I feel as though I finished a barrel on my own. It's strange because they're mead is far weaker than ours."

Erik chuckled before kissing the top of her head.

"My love, they mixed that mead with whisky. I thought you knew, so I didn't stop you from drinking more than me. You've drunk me under the table before."

"Oh." Freya struggled to make sense of what Erik said as the effects took hold of her foggy mind.

Erik stood them up and helped her to the stairs. It surprised him that his inebriated bride still walked even though he knew she could not focus. He knew if she was sober, she would object to him carrying her up the stairs, but he was not about to risk her tumbling and breaking her neck. He scooped her into his arms, and she nestled into his chest.

"Thank you for taking care of me. I adore you," her words were soft and slurred.

"Always. I adore you too."

They reached Freya's chamber which was now theirs together. He stood her up and stripped away her clothes before tucking her into bed. She propped herself onto one arm as she watched Erik undress.

"I have the most gorgeous and well-made husband. Such a fine body. I shall enjoy playing with it for the rest of time. I would taste every single bit. Did you know my husband is delicious?"

Erik laughed as he listened to his drunk wife ramble. He slipped in beside her and pulled the cover over them. Freya wriggled closer, and Erik indulged her as his body sprang awake. He had been sure she would fall asleep as soon as she made it under the cover, but he was most certainly wrong.

"I thought you were tired."

"I was. You woke me up."

Erik captured her under her arms and hauled her up to cover his body. He stroked her head and pulled her hair aside so he could caress her back.

"I am the most fortunate man. How did I ever come to deserve you?"

When Freya did not answer, he looked down and found she had drifted off. He shifted, and her eyes fluttered open.

"You're you. That's all I need." Freya murmured before falling into a deep sleep.

Erik covered them once again and enjoyed the feel of Freya tucked against him as she settled in her sleep. It was not long before he fell asleep with Freya's honey-scented skin filling his nostrils.

CHAPTER THIRTEEN

Morning came all too soon, but once again Freya awoke knowing she slept better than she ever did before sharing a bed with Erik. They dressed and grabbed bannocks, oatcakes Freya would never come to like, on their way to the stables. Freya was glad to escape the watching and judgmental eyes of Erik's clan and thanked the gods once more that he was Norse and only a relative to these Highlanders.

Freya, Erik, and their crew rode out with Alex and his two score of guardsmen. They traveled for three days, stopping when the horses required it or it was no longer safe to travel in the dark. They passed outlying villages and farms where the residents came out to greet their laird. A few told stories that a band of Norsemen were traveling through the area looking for young men and young women. This last piece of news raised several eyebrows. Freya scowled, knowing Inga's ring of women had not been limited to the island. She found an even greater personal motivation. She knew she might have been able to fight her way out of captivity should someone foolishly try to trap her as a thrall, but most women would not. They needed someone who would fight for them. She also knew these were not conquered women, but women tricked into believing they were getting a better opportunity with a husband and land.

"We spotted them a day ago," one of Alex's scouts rode back to the group. He had ridden to a village to the south of where their larger party made their way inland. "They are on MacLeod land, but just over the border."

"I wonder if Laird MacLeod knows there are Norsemen poaching his clan." Alex's jaw set as his eyes scanned the horizon. He turned in his saddled to call forward three men. "Allen, Robert, and Tavish, ride to the

MacLeod keep and inform the laird of what is happening. Be cautious before you reveal too much. I doubt he would condone this, but on the off chance he does, don't play our hand."

The three men took off heading west as the rest of the group continued a more southerly path. Erik was on alert. Something did not feel right the further south they traveled. The hair on the back of his neck prickled, and when he looked to Freya, he knew she sensed the same thing. She held her reins loosely in one hand while the other rested on the hilt of one of her knives. They exchanged a speculative look, and Erik shook his head.

"Do ye smell ambush in the air," Alex cut in.

"We do," Erik scanned the horizon as Freya turned to look behind them. "Something just doesn't feel right. It's as though someone is watching us, but there is nowhere for anyone to hide. We're in the open which makes us easy targets, but we can see for leagues. There is no one else around."

With no enemy to see, they carried on ever vigilant. It was after dusk when they stopped for the night. Everyone was still on edge. The sense of impending doom settled over all the riders as the day progressed. They agreed not to build any fires that night and ate only dried beef and bannocks. Freya and Erik laid out their bedrolls head to head as they had the previous nights. Erik stood talking to Alex when Freya slipped into the woods to find some privacy. She was not far from camp when she heard a rustling in the brush. She inched towards a wide tree trunk and pressed her back against it. She heard voices but the sound was too far away to discern the words. She crept from one tree to another as she neared the voices. She saw the glow of a small fire before she could see the men who sat around it. Freya scanned her options and spotted just the right perch to observe without being seen. She knew she did not have long before Erik noticed her absence and would search. Without a sound, Freya pulled herself into the low branches of a tree that stood as close to the camp as she dared. She pulled herself on her belly onto a long limb. Freya could see and hear clearly. A group of fifteen men sat around the fire, but from the extra bedrolls she could tell there must have been closer to twenty. She could tell two were asleep, and the others were most likely hunting. Freya considered how she had gotten so close without their watch noticing. She worried that she just trapped herself because the watch had, in fact, seen her and they were letting her hang there like bait. She wondered why the men wore what looked like plaids, but they had no distinguishable pattern or colors. Her mind skipped from one question to another as she listened. The men were a ragtag band with filthy faces and mouths.

"We attack just before dawn. They won't be expecting that after we've left them alone this long. They sensed something earlier, but they will be more complacent now. We shall go when they are still sleeping. We cut down their bluidy watch, slit their throats if ye must, and then we move onto the laird and those bastard Norse. The bitch with the long hair is mine."

The clear leader of the group stroked a scar that ran from his temple along his cheekbone, cutting the edge of his eye, and down to the center of his lips before crossing to his chin. It was a nasty scar that had not healed, disfiguring the man's face with no way to disguise it. Freya remembered giving it to the man many years ago. Leif led a mission along the eastern coast of Scotland that took them close to the English border. There had been a fierce battle where Freya got separated from the others when they swept through a castle and its kirk. Freya encountered four men who surrounded her. She had lashed out at the first man who stepped near her while throwing her knife at another. She had not even planned the strike before swinging her sword. It had made contact and sliced diagonally across the man's face. She had pulled back and moved on to the next fighter until she could get away. She was sure she had killed all four men. She slit the other three throats, but left assuming the man would bleed out from his wounds. He had not, and now he held a grudge.

"Hakin never said anything about fighting them here. We're supposed to keep recruiting other lawless men until we have enough to fill his boats. Then we fight near Hakin's home. His purpose is to gain land. Fight them here, and all we have is twice the number of battles and twice the chance to get killed. We fight where Hakin paid us to fight." One man stood before the leader while several others nodded.

"And Grímr pays us to do as he says. Hakin may supply most of the coin, but the extra Grímr pays makes us loyal to him. He said we kill them whenever we have the chance. We have the chance now. I'm in charge here, little brother, unless you wish to fight me too."

Freya watched the two men stand off before the younger man nodded once.

"I'll remind you of this decision when we're walking through the fires of hell before the midday meal tomorrow."

The leader laughed and the ripple spread through the camp until all the men were laughing and slapping their knees. Freya used the opportunity to work her way back to the ground. She was sure and light-footed. She raced back through the trees and bushes until she spotted Erik looking around in panic.

"I'm right here," she called to him.

Erik yanked her none too gently into his arms.

"I was calling to you, but you didn't answer, and then I couldn't find you. We were just about to search for you."

"I know, and I'm sorry, but I couldn't turn up the opportunity that landed in my lap. I heard some noises and followed it to a camp near here. I found some of the mercenaries there."

Erik wanted to shake her for putting herself at risk while hugging her for finding what they searched for.

"I climbed into a tree to listen and watch. There's about fifteen, and they are wearing breeches with plaids I couldn't recognize. There is no pattern, and they look black. The leader's brother said something about them being lawless men. They've been banished, so no wonder they will work for whoever pays the most. They're supposed to find other men like them."

"You took an unnecessary risk, Freya. They could have found you and either taken you or killed you on the spot." Erik's heart pounded as she relayed what she learned, and he realized how much danger she had put herself in.

"Oh, they would have killed me on the spot. I have no doubt about that." Freya stated as she tried to pull away.

"How do you know that? Freya, what haven't you told me yet?"

"I was going to mention the rest when we talk to Alex, but this part doesn't matter if he hears it. The leader is a man I fought several years ago. I thought I'd left him for dead. I guess not since he's planning his revenge. He intends to kill me." Freya's frank tone grated on Erik's raw nerves.

"You don't seem that concerned. Clearly you didn't manage to kill him last time. What makes you think you'll succeed this time?"

Freya froze as though Erik dumped ice water over her. Her reasonable mind knew he spoke from fear, but her emotional mind won as it had so many times before with their battle of words.

"When you see his scar, you will understand why I thought he would bleed to death. I killed the other three I fought alongside him. I shouldn't have been so merciful, but I was younger. Fear not, my love, I have little mercy left."

She pulled away from him and stepped around him. Erik did not know if he should let her go or stop her to clear the air. He chose the latter and caught her arm just above the elbow.

"Wait," he murmured. Erik flinched at the cold stare she turned on him. He was not looking at the woman who made passionate love to him. He was looking at a warrior who had no time for sentimentality. "I'll never stop worrying about you. Accept that now. It's why I fight next to you and with you. I just want you to be cautious."

Erik stepped forward and leaned to whisper in her ear.

"I have no reason to carry on if I lose you. You are my everything."

Freya took a deep inhale and blew it out as the tension slid from her body.

"I know I shouldn't have sounded so flippant. I just didn't want you to worry about me. Then it felt like you doubted me. I didn't like that." Freya's voice trailed off.

"We still have a great deal to learn about how to communicate with one another without arguing. We'll get there. Just not tonight." Erik grinned.

"I suppose not. Erik, we need to speak to Alex. They are planning an ambush."

"I figured as much."

Freya and Erik walked to Alex, and Freya relayed what she knew including her history with the leader.

"Aye, so this is personal, is it? He's holding a grudge like an old man, a bodach."

"Yes, so he will target me while his men fight the rest of you. I think his brother is the voice of reason and will try to convince him to take me alive. He wants to watch me draw my last breath. I suspect the scar damaged some of his vision. There's no way it couldn't have. I know what I did, and I plan to take advantage of that. If I can position myself where he can't see me clearly, then I'll be able to end this quickly. If not," Freya shrugged, "it'll take me a little longer, but either way, I will walk away knowing I slit his throat."

"Bloodthirsty little Valkyrie you have there, Cousin."

"Don't I know it. I'm just glad she's no longer out for mine."

Freya shook her head as she looked at both of them.

"I don't know if you two plan to stay up gossiping like two little old women, but I intend to get what sleep I can."

Alex and Erik watched her walk away before exchanging looks.

"I dinna ken if I should envy ye or worry for ye."

"Envy me for sure, Cousin. She is worth every bit of frustration she causes me because the reward couldn't be better."

Erik made his way to his bedroll and extended his arm over his head to Freya. She took his hand as they both eased into slumber.

The entire camp was on alert as the sky lightened from the dark dead of night to the light blue of predawn. The stars faded as the moon gave way to its celestial partner. All the warriors were awake with their swords gripped beneath the covers of their bedrolls. Alex's archers were in the trees above them. The watch was posted just beyond the shadows cast by the fire. No one spoke, and no one moved. Their alertness allowed them to hear the men approach. Their attackers were silent, but they were prepared. One watchman gave the owl call warning that had them springing to their feet weapons drawn. It was only moments later that a battle cry went out from the lawless band and Alex's men responded with the Mackay war cry, calling out for the White Banner of Mackay. The melee ensued with clashes of steel, grunts, and cries of pain. Freya and Erik surged forward and angled themselves to fight back to back. Erik kept an eye on Alex until he saw him fight alongside his second. Focused on keeping his head and helping Freya defend them, he saw the man Freya described edge around the outer circle of the battle. Erik could see he was looking for his opportunity to rush Freya.

"I see him," she called over the clatter of her sword against her opponent. "He's looking for a way in rather than fighting like the rest of his men. Coward!" She called out.

"Freya," Erik hissed.

"I want this over. Let him come for me."

Erik once again was torn between loving the bravery that made Freya who she was and wanting to throttle her for her daredevil heart.

Freya's voice carried and an angry bellow traveled back to them.

"Bitch, ye breathe yer last."

"Only after I give a scar to match the first one I gave you."

Freya twisted away from Erik and swung her sword with both hands. She was stronger than she had been years earlier. Stronger, more experienced, and with more to live for, she took the man off guard. He stumbled back, and Freya followed up her first strike with a flurry of strokes as her blade nicked his sides and drew blood. But never enough to kill. She taunted him as she went on the offensive rather than the defensive. She angled him toward the fire. He found his footing and retaliated with the force Freya remembered. She also remembered how he fought. She knew the openings to look for. She shifted her sword into her left hand and disconcerted him long enough to flick a knife from the bracer at her wrist. Freya struck out and sliced a matching line across the opposite side of his face. The scarred man leaped backwards into the fire. He stumbled as his breeches caught fire. He jumped free of the flames, but his pants were already burning. He had to choose between putting out his pants or fighting Freya. Her opponent tried to back away, but she followed. Freya thrust her sword into his gut before plunging her knife into his neck. She raised her booted foot and kicked him back into the fire. She spun away as the first acrid whiffs of burning flesh reached her nostrils.

"Ye are a bloodthirsty wench," Alex called out.

Freya grinned as she returned to her spot next to Erik. He angled himself to shield Freya from the two approaching men as she caught her breath. By the time the first man swung, Freya was once again twisting and thrusting as her sword sliced through the second man's ribs. It was only moments later that the skirmish ended.

Freya wiped the sweat from her brow as she looked around and surveyed the injuries to her crew. The Norse warriors came out with a few scrapes. A handful of Alex's men had minor injuries, but they were all still standing. Freya scanned the ground and found the man who spoke out against the leader. She walked over and toed him with her booted foot. He groaned and his eyes fluttered open.

"Be sure to look for your brother in the flames of hell when you meet for that midday meal. Make sure he remembers I am the one who sent him there."

The man drew a ragged inhale and shuddered it out. He licked his lips as he tried to form words. It tempted Freya to lean forward to hear better, but she knew this could all be a trick to get her to expose her neck.

"If you have something to say, try harder. You are already a dead man. You are on borrowed time."

"No clan helping Hakin. Only lawless men. He's getting desperate because none of the clans will help. Grímr holds the purse, but his wife controls the coin." The last rasping exhale whistled through the man's teeth before his sightless eyes stared at Freya. She walked over to the leader again and kicked him in the gut. When there was no movement, she bent low and saw the same sightless eyes she saw moments ago. Both were dead. Neither was a concern anymore.

"So, what now?" Alex asked after checking on all his men.

Freya watched as one of her crew bandaged a shallow gash on another's arm. She turned to look at Erik and shrugged.

"We haven't accomplished anything. This was more of a hiccup. Until we find Hakin and Grímr, or perhaps even more importantly Inga, we aren't done."

"She's right. We continue on until we have something more to take back to tell our fathers."

"Very well. Let us leave this place. The carrion can have them."

CHAPTER FOURTEEN

The riders mounted before the sky was even pink. They rode hard as they neared the place where the three clans' territories met. Alex slowed them as they approached their own patrol.

"Laird, we didna think to see ye all the way out here. But glad we are that ye sent Keith when ye did. I take it he told ye aboot the camp nay far from here."

"We came to see for ourselves."

"Aye, we've had our eye on it. It's on MacLeod land, but the Sutherlands are aware too. The MacLeods sent a man back to their laird just two days ago. It's one of the few things we've all been able to agree on. Better than just staring at one another as we patrol the border."

"How far is it?"

"Aboot an hour's ride south."

The sound of approaching riders from two directions made them look around. Freya and Erik were wary, but Alex grinned.

"That's the fastest I've ever seen a Sutherland or a MacLeod move," he boomed. "Spying on us, are ye?"

Ten men from each neighboring clan rode towards them but stopped a safe distance.

"Laird Mackay, always a pleasure to see ye."

"Is that ye, Kenneth? Ye've grown, lad. Ye must be the size of yer da, and he's a bluidy mountain." Alex looked at the foreigners and explained, "he's the MacLeod laird's heir. His oldest son."

"Dinna forget aboot me, Mackay." Called a deep baritone from the opposite direction.

"Christ's bones! Is that ye, Andrew Sutherland? What do they feed ye lads? I'm feeling positively decrepit," Alex joked even though neither man could have been more than five years his junior. He nodded to the Sutherland heir.

"I take it ye're here aboot our unwanted visitors," Kenneth MacLeod motioned his men forward. "What are they to ye?"

Kenneth seemed to notice the group of blond foreigners for the first time. He launched another set of questions before waiting for answers to his first.

"Ye're marauding cousin's come to visit, has he? Planning to raid us from inland rather than the coast?"

"Play nicely, Kenneth. And it's nae ma cousin Alex ye should worry aboot but ma bonny new cousin, Freya. She'll chew ye up, spit ye out, and grind ye to the ground."

Andrew Sutherland rode up and looked over Freya.

"She's too bonny to be so fierce. She looks as sweet as treacle."

"*She* is like one of your thistles. Pretty to look at, but will leave a sting," Freya piped in. "And *she* is wed."

Erik leaned over and kissed the cheek she proffered.

The men chuckled as Freya teasingly glowered.

"All kidding aside, we are here to scout the Norsemen who took up roots on yer land, MacLeod. They're searching for and hiring mercenaries from the surrounding area. They found success on Orkney, but we've learned neither of yer clans are helping." Alex brought them back to the reason why they were speaking.

Kenneth MacLeod and Andrew Sutherland crossed their arms and huffed, duly insulted.

"Settle. We had to check. Hakin and his brother, Grímr, are hiring any clanless men they can find, and I suspect any of yer poorest tenant farmers are their other targets. They may also steal lasses to enslave and trade."

Kenneth and Andrew sat astride their mounts stunned.

"We suspected nefarious intentions, but we didna ken they were looking to poach our clan members." Andrew shook his head.

"We've had peace among our three clans, and I wasna sure what to make of this. I'm relieved that we're all in agreement that this ends now. Or at least I assume that's what we all intend." Kenneth gave a hard stare at Alex and Andrew.

"Of course, it is. That's why I'm talking to ye both. It was lucky for us ye're both patrolling yer own borders. I would ask that ye send a few of yer men with us for the numbers and so we have an eyewitness to what happens. Do ye both agree?"

"Aye, but I'll be part of that group," Kenneth spoke up.

"As will I," answered Andrew.

"Hold on. What will yer father's say? I amnae looking to have either of them come chasing me when either of ye gets a wee scratch."

Andrew grinned as he looked at Freya then looked to Alex. "Why do ye think he sent me out here? The lasses love scars, and he says I'm too pretty."

"I always thought ye looked like a lass," Kenneth lobbed back.

"We can't sit here all day. Can we leave these two to compare their cocks, and the rest of the adults ride out?" Freya huffed. She had been around enough male posturing to satisfy a lifetime. If they would not be searching from Grímr and Hakin, then she would rather spend her time with Erik. Sitting on a horse in the sun listening to these two trade barbs was like listening to her brother and cousin go at it. She was not interested.

Three scores pairs of eyes turned towards her. She was unrepentant.

"You know that is what they are doing. I'm bored. Let's ride." Freya nudged her horse forward. "Someone lead or I will figure it out myself."

Erik laughed as he kneed his horse to ride alongside Freya's. He grinned over his shoulder at Kenneth.

"See, I'm not the marauding one."

The combined group rode south for three quarters of an hour and only slowed when Kenneth gave the signal they were close. The leaders had devised a plan as they rode. Freya, Erik, and their crew knew who they were looking for. They would scout first to see if either Hakin or Grímr were in the camp and then, once they knew the numbers they faced, they would ride back to the others. None of the patrols knew how large the camp was, so Freya and Erik knew they were riding in blind. Neither wanted to engage until they had proper reinforcements, but they also knew Hakin and Grímr's strategies when it came to setting guards. They might not get close enough to learn anything without getting themselves discovered.

"Cousin, remember to stay within earshot. You know how loud I can whistle, but I don't want to wait long if I need you. My mother wouldn't forgive you if I came back with any wee scratches." Erik smirked.

"The last thing I need is Lorna coming for me. Ye dinna need to fash." Alex chuckled.

Freya looked between the men.

"I still need to tell you the story of how my parents met." Erik smiled at Freya. "I think it would be the perfect bedtime story."

"If I can stay awake that long. You seem to know just how to put me to bed." Freya's gaze swept over Erik's body as she licked her lips. Erik felt heat shoot straight to his groin, which now painfully rested against his saddle.

"Save that for later, lovebirds. We dinna need to listen to yer newlywed chatter."

"Just wait yer turn." Erik laughed as he and Freya led their crew towards the enemy camp.

CHAPTER FIFTEEN

It took less than a quarter of an hour to reach the camp. They had been much closer than they realized.

"It's a good thing we didn't give ourselves away," Erik whispered.

The others nodded. The group fanned out as they approached on foot. They had tied their horses close enough to escape in a hurry, but far enough away so that the mounts in the camp could not hear or smell their horses. The crew crept forward as they slipped past trees and bushes. It was one of Erik's warriors who signaled first that he could see movement. They continued to creep until they were all but upon the outlaws. In the center of the camp sat Grímr. He looked pale and weakened, but he barked out orders as though he was still in battle form. Freya and the others hunkered down to observe. It was not long before Grímr stood and moved about the camp. There was a restlessness about him as he limped from one small group of men to another. The men, for their part, were engaged in various tasks. Some were sharpening weapons or repairing those in need. Others were preparing food for what would be the evening meal. There were a few women scattered about helping with the food preparation. They set the camp up near a flowing stream, so some of the women were laundering clothes. Erik pointed further downstream to where there were at least a score of men bathing. It was clear these were Norsemen from both their fair hair and their willingness to remain in the frigid water. Freya counted close to a hundred men there. As her eyes took in more of the camp, she realized she would describe it as more of a small village. Freya pointed out the fletcher who had several assistants as he restrung bows and ordered his helpers to make new arrows. Freya's crew members were to her left, and their movement caught her attention. They pointed further to their left, but

Freya could not tell what they saw. It was only a few moments later that she realized her crew was not pointing out something so much as warning them. Someone had spotted them.

Erik and Freya looked at one another and shook their heads. They did not have nearly enough people to stand a fighting chance. Erik and Freya, along with their crew members, retreated as they faded back into the woods. They could hear the cries going up, and they heard Grímr's booming voice demanding to know what was happening. The entire retreating group heard someone bellow Freya's name. Erik shifted to run behind Freya covering her back. There was no opportunity for Freya to argue with Erik, but Erik saw the set of her shoulders shift and knew he would hear from his beautiful bride once they made it to safety. He would listen to anything she had to say if it meant she was safe enough to say it.

They reached the horses just as the first wave of men broke through the trees behind them. They were quick to mount as arrows flew over their heads. Each of the riders set their shields over their backs and ducked their heads low as they charged towards the Highlanders waiting for them.

Erik sounded a loud whistle as they made haste away from their pursuers. They reached the Highlanders who were spurring their horses. Freya felt several arrows thunk against her shield, but none felt like they stuck. She looked towards Erik and saw three sticking from his shield. Fear and anger tempted her to turn back to avenge the attack on her husband, but she did not have a death wish that day. She glanced about and saw that their crew was uninjured, but several arrows stuck out of their shields. It was not long before the band outrode the reach of their pursuers who were on foot. But none of them slowed, knowing, undoubtedly, that there would be more pursuers close behind on horseback.

"We ride into the hills," Andrew called. "Some of them might know their way aboot them, but none of them grew up in them like we did." He gestured to his men.

No one argued the merit of getting lost in the foothills, as there were plenty of twisting trails, caves, and small hidey-holes that would offer them shelter. Riders unfamiliar with the terrain would either get lost or believe the land was untraversable.

The sure-footed Highland ponies with their shaggy coats and large hooves led the charge, while the Norse stallions and geldings had little trouble keeping up on their longer legs trained on ice and snow.

"Erik, Freya, ye and yers stay close. The terrain shifts with the loose shale at the foot of the hills then the ledges become vera narrow. Keep us in yer sights."

"Freya rides in the middle," Erik called out. Before she could argue, "It's not a suggestion."

Once again, he knew he would hear about his highhandedness later, but he would gladly listen knowing she survived to yell at him.

The three score Highlanders branched off as each clan took a different approach to the hills. There was no way such a large group could make it through the passes and remain hidden. Erik followed Freya as they picked their way over the loose rocks and climbed. They had not gotten far when Freya heard Erik's horse release a loud neigh that made her own horse edgy. She looked back to see the horse dancing around and refusing to move forward. The horse skittered about and looked ready to rear. Erik was trying to control the animal, but the path was not wide enough to allow the horse to move away from the edge. Freya put her own reins in her teeth, leaving them as slack as she could, as she twisted and stretched to catch Erik's horse's bridle. Her own horse took two steps back at the tug on his bit. That small shift gave Freya enough leverage to grip the bridle in two hands and tug downwards. Erik's horse tried to rear and nearly lifted Freya out of the saddle, but as she squeezed her knees to keep her balance, her horse thought he was supposed to walk forward. Once again, the shift in her own horse's position gave her the leverage she needed to help control Erik's. She kept tugging downwards on the bridle until all four hooves were on the ground and the horse was once again following hers.

Freya let go and spun forward regaining her seat. She could not bring herself to look over the edge to see how far they climbed, to see how far Erik would have fallen if he and his horse had gone over the edge. She felt a sense of fear she had not known since her early battles. A lump formed in her throat she thought might choke her. She swallowed over and over as she wheezed.

"Freya?" Erik sounded as distraught as she felt.

She nodded her head until she could clear her voice enough to speak.

"Now I understand why you wanted me to ride in front of you. You needed me to lead your arse to safety. It's a good thing it's such a fine arse, or I might have left you behind."

Erik's hollow laugh echoed in her ears. Erik and Freya both knew neither was going to talk about their emotions to anyone, not each other or those around them. It had terrified them.

The remainder of the ride into the hills was less eventful, but everyone was on guard for falling rocks and pursuers.

"Do we dare stop?" Erik addressed Alex. He spoke in hushed tones since the hills echoed, but the horses needed resting. "If we push the horses much more, at least one is bound to go lame."

"Aye. I ken. If we can just make it to the next pass, then the hills will protect us for a good while. I dinna think any of those mercenaries are as familiar with this area as we are, so they will either be slow or give up the chase. Hopefully, the latter."

It was another half an hour before the riders reined in. The pass was narrow, so it was impossible for those at the front of the line to speak to those in the rear. Each rider passed back information, but eventually all the riders dismounted. Alex led them around the corner, and Freya gasped when she saw a small loch tucked away. She never would have guessed it was there, but she was thankful for it. It would be freshwater, so animals and humans alike could rest and drink. She led her horse to the shore and watched as the others spread out with their mounts. Many squatted on the shore and cupped their hands to drink or splash water on their heated face and neck. Erik guided his stallion towards Freya's, but kept them a safe distance apart. The animals were used to each other now, but they had a love/hate relationship that often involved nipping and stomping. The space between the animals offered them some privacy. Freya launched herself into his arms and trembled as she felt his reassuring embrace prop her up. He lifted her chin and saw the glisten of tears she tried to blink away. His mouth lowered to hers as he took in the pink cheeks, the tousled hair, and the braids that were coming loose. He inhaled fresh air mingled with honey. He absorbed the comfort of her in his arms as it soaked straight to his soul. All his other senses satisfied, he allowed himself to taste her. The kiss was born of love, desperation, and relief all intertwined to create a conflagration of need. Need they both knew would go unsatisfied for the foreseeable future, but it was enough to come together for at least a kiss.

"I have never been so frightened in all my life. I don't know when my heart will beat again because it felt like it stopped when I thought you were going over that ledge. I praise All Father for keeping you alive. I don't know what I would do without you." Freya's lower lip trembled when they pulled apart. "That was worse than seeing you in any battle."

"That was not something I ever want to experience again. It frightened me more that the horse would pull you from your saddle and then you'd be trampled or flung off the ledge. Part of me wants to worship every inch of you in thanksgiving for your help and another part of me wants to turn you over my knee for risking your own life."

"The very next time we are alone, you can do both."

They sank back into each other's arms for another kiss that soothed both of their nerves but only heightened their desire.

"If we don't stop now, I will haul you over my shoulder and find a large trunk to hide behind while I maul you." Erik growled.

Freya exaggerated her glance as she looked around.

"I don't see any trees, but I've always wanted to make love in the water. Since that bath got cut short--" she trailed off.

"If we were alone. But there is no chance in this lifetime or the next that any of these men are going to see you undress or come out of the water with your tunic stuck to you like a second skin. Alex would leave here, if I didn't kill him too, with none of his guardsmen."

"Fine. You're not being much fun." Freya laughed and stuck out her tongue.

"I shall remind you of that and show you how you can use that luscious tongue of yours when we do get some privacy." Erik laughed along with her but grew serious again. "Freya, I love you. Don't risk yourself like that again for me. If you'd died saving me, and I was left without you, I can't imagine how desolate my life would be."

"You say the most utterly ridiculous things for such an intelligent man. You would leave me a widow? What life would I have now I know I love you? Things are no different than before. We both fight to save one another whether it's on the battlefield or some bloody ledge. That's just how it is."

"Ever practical if nothing else. Fine. My point is, I can't imagine a life without you. I love you that much."

"I feel the same. Even if you still annoy me with the unreasonable things you say." Freya pecked a kiss on his cheek before leading her horse away from the water.

Freya took three steps before a cry went up, and she looked around. She saw dust rising from the trail they took to find the loch. She squinted to make out whether it was members of the Sutherland or MacLeod clan or worse, Grímr's men. As the first men came around the final bend, Freya could not see any plaids.

"Erik, we ride! It's Grímr!"

They were both mounted in a matter of seconds just as the rest of the Mackays. Alex was pointing to a flat expanse that rapped around one side of the lake.

"Hurry!" the laird called out. "Each man takes the path he can reach but ride in pairs at least. We meet back at the bottom of the hills. Freya and Erik, ye ride with me."

CHAPTER SIXTEEN

Freya sat low over her horse's withers as she and Erik charged after Alex. She had no opportunity to look around, and she did not dare look behind her. All she could hear was the stomping of hooves as the Mackays surged forward and Grímr's men gave chase. Erik followed behind Freya, keeping her in his sights, but he looked back and caught sight of Grímr himself leading the fray.

"He's with them!" Erik yelled over the barrage of sounds. "Grímr's leading them."

That was all Erik got out as they reached another narrow slope that would bring them out of the hills. This time Erik's horse sensed the urgency and behaved. They were on level and solid ground only moments later. Alex led them across a meadow that would give them the opportunity to spread out so all the riders could gain distance between themselves and the band of mercenaries. It also put them in the wide open.

"Targes!" Alex's voice spread through the group, and the riders swung their shields onto their back. A volley of arrows rained down on them. None did any damage, but it was a sure sign that there was little distance between prey and predator.

"We can't ride like this the entire time back to the keep. That's three days from here." Freya looked to Alex who rode to her left and then Erik who rode to her right.

"We willna. We arenae far from Castle Iruill. It's on ma land. We can shelter there with reinforcements until these men tire and run back to MacLeod land. Then we can make our way back to Varrich."

"And from there we sail," Freya was emphatic. Erik was in agreement. It was time for them to leave Scotland and get home to their tribes with both the news and the bounty they found.

It was a hard ride for the next hour while they gained then lost distance between them and their pursuers. It surprised Freya they were willing to give chase so far from their camp. She knew Grímr had plans to murder her, Leif, and Erik as the heirs to Ivar and Rangvald. It would be the only way for him to gain the land their tribes now held, but he surprised her by letting his desire to see them dead override his sense. He would waste time having to double back to break down his camp.

Unless he left men to do that or he doesn't care. We still need to know where his boats are. Where did he come ashore? Wherever that is, we need to be far, far away.

"There!" Alex called pointing to a growing speck in the distance. As they approached, they could see a tower surrounded by a high curtain wall. It was not large, but it looked well made and well defended.

The horses must have sensed how close they were to their destination, because they all seemed to dredge up a last burst of energy as they sprinted towards the tower.

They could hear the bells ringing and saw movement on the battlement as Alex held up a piece of plaid to signal who approached. The portcullis rose and they dashed below it before it fell back into place. The horses clattered into the bailey as stable boys rushed out to corral the lathered beasts. Alex swung down and charged up the steps to the battlements, disappearing as he called out orders. Freya and Erik checked with their crew and Alex's warriors to be sure none of the arrows had found homes in any of them.

"Thank All Father not a single one of us came out of that injured." Erik looked around before making his own way to the battlements with Freya on his heels. They could see for miles once they reached the top of the curtain wall. Grímr's men stopped just outside the range of Alex's archers. They could see Grímr, but he was too far away to read his expression. They could, however, see he still wore a bandage at the thigh, and one of his arms hung limp.

"How did he manage to hang on for that entire ride?" Freya muttered.

"Hatred is a great motivator," Erik quipped.

They stood staring until Grímr whipped his mount around and the outlaws turned northwest and back towards both MacLeod land and the coast.

"I'm sure they've given up their pursuit now, but they're headed to their boats." Erik observed. "We must do the same, and faster than them."

"Agreed, Cousin. We rest here for the night, then ride out early in the morning. I will have men scout to be sure they arenae lying in wait for us, but I suspect ye are right. His fit of temper is over, and now he is scheming again."

"How far are we still from Varrich?"

"A good two days of riding, but once we get to Loch Kuntaill, ye can use several of the birlins in the village of Keanloch. The only thing in our favor is Grímr will have to travel further to get to his boats."

"You mean we could have sailed part of the way rather than ridden for three days?" Freya's eyebrows flew to her hairline.

"Nae with all our horses. Ye and yer crew will go since there are so few of ye. The rest of us will have to ride."

Freya looked contrite, knowing she and her crew were lucky to make better time than Alex and his men. It also meant they would arrive at Varrich without an escort. She hoped Erik's standing was strong enough for the clan to welcome them without Alex there to serve as host and sponsor.

"Dinna fash, lass. They will treat ye well and give ye supplies for yer voyage." Alex grinned, "if for nae other reason than the lasses are in love with Erik and will do aught to please him, and they'll be glad to see the tail end of ye since ye snagged the lad."

Freya's mouth drew into a pursed line.

"Thank the gods for small mercies."

Erik chuckled and pulled her against him to whisper.

"The sooner we get to Varrich, the sooner I can make love to you again. The sooner we get to your boat, the sooner we are in your cabin, and I can make love to you over and over."

Erik's murmured words mollified Freya as a tingle spread through her, and she leaned into Erik's large frame as his body made her feel protected. She had not realized just how the anxiety of the past day was wearing on her. Freya turned and rested her forehead against Erik's chest and closed her eyes. She pulled her hands up between them and gripped his tunic.

She surprised Erik with this rare moment of public vulnerability. He ran his hands over Freya's back with a bewildered look at Alex over her head. Alex shrugged.

"Mayhap ye newlyweds would like to take yer carrying on to a chamber. I am sure my chatelaine has already prepared them. I will see to yer crew."

Erik nodded, but Freya did not budge.

"Freya, let's go inside," Erik's hushed voice permeated the fog that had settled over Freya's mind.

She allowed him to guide her inside, and they followed an older woman who spoke little but showed them a well-appointed chamber. Freya stepped inside and unclasped her cloak and unbuttoned her vest. She found a stool and sat to take off her boots while Erik requested a bath be brought up for them. Once her boots were off, she went to stand by the window and looked out of the meadow they crossed to arrive at the tower. There was nothing to see whereas only a short while ago, there had been a sea of warriors racing across it and then a tense standoff. Erik approached with hesitation because he had never seen Freya so introspective and pensive. He was not sure if she wanted him beside her or if it would be better to give her space, but when she reached out a hand behind her, he clasped her shoulders and pulled her against his chest. She leaned against him as he wrapped his arms around her.

"What's troubling you?" he murmured.

"Everything. We've known peace among our clans for years, and now Hakin and Grímr are determined to destroy it. The fight is pointless. Our tribes will win even with them replenishing their army. Our warriors keep killing more of them than they do us, but what a waste of our people. We have taken their coins and set free their source of trade. Hakin may have even discovered that by now since he wasn't with Grímr. We still haven't found Inga, and we must sail home knowing that Hakin may have pirates set to raid any boat that goes by. Even with these setbacks, we are still ahead. We have lost none of our land, and Hakin has no homestead left. Yet we must keep fighting. Erik, I'm tired. I already was tiring of the constant expeditions, but now we're wed, and I want us to stay home long enough to create an actual home. I want time to enjoy being married to you without worrying one of us will die. We still need to have the actual ceremony. I'll keep fighting because that's who I am. I am a shieldmaiden. But I would like a reprieve."

Freya continued to look out the window for a few more moments before turning in Erik's arms and once again resting her head on his chest. Erik understood Freya with a weariness they shared. She spoke all the things he felt. The war with Hakin and Grímr was pointless. It was a vendetta and nothing more at this point. He wanted to go home and fall into bed with Freya and wake up to her every morning knowing they weren't in danger and would live to enjoy another sunset and sunrise together. They might not be ready to have children yet, but they were each other's family now. He wanted to enjoy it.

Erik kissed the top of her head as a knock came at the door. He was unwilling to let her go long enough to answer it, so instead he called, "Come in."

Servants entered with a tub that was far smaller than the one at Varrich, but there were plenty of buckets of steamy water. They filled the tub silently and left just as quietly. Erik helped Freya undress and walked her to the tub. Freya sank into the water and sighed. She slipped low enough to dunk her head before coming up and resting it against the edge. She had to sit with her legs bent, so she could not imagine how Erik would fit. He would have to dangle his legs over the sides.

"There certainly isn't room for two," Erik quipped. He dunked a linen into the water and lathered it with soap. "Sit forward."

Erik ran the linen over Freya's back as he rubbed the kinks from her shoulders. He felt them relax, but the knots below her skin did not budge. He ran the linen on her arms before lathering it again and running it between her breasts. Freya's eyes drifted closed as she arched her back to him. Erik trailed the square over each breast following it with his bare hand. He massaged the fleshy orbs and watched as her nipples puckered. There was fire blazing in the hearth, so it was not chilly air that hardened them. He leaned forward and took one into his mouth. Freya's responding mewl made his cock twitch and his tight leather pants became unbearable. He released her long enough to shuck his clothes. He kneeled naked beside the tub. Freya's soapy hand reached out to cup his neck as he leaned back over to worship the other breast. Freya's breath caught as Erik slid his hand below the surface of the water to glide between her thighs. He nudged them apart, and Freya let them fall as wide as the tub allowed. Dissatisfied, she lifted her feet onto the edge. Erik continued his mission and washed her entrance until her hips swayed and the water rippled. He let the linen go and replaced it with his fingers. He trailed his fingers along her netherlips as Freya's breath hitched and a sound of pleading came from her.

"Not yet, my love."

She whimpered, and Erik showed her an ounce of mercy as one finger slipped inside. Freya tried to angle her hips to offer him greater ease. Erik's hand that had still been working her breasts slid behind her head to support her as he devoured her. He breathed her in and lured her tongue to his mouth where they tangled together. Freya's breasts felt heavy and prickled while her core ached. The need for him to give her more consumed her. Reading her silent cues, Erik thrust his fingers inside and stroked. Freya looped her arms around his neck and pulled her feet back into the tub to push down, bringing her hips higher. The ache now tormented her as it became a scalding burn within her belly.

"Erik," she begged against his lips.

"Not yet."

"I can't," her whimper gave Erik pause. He pulled his head away to look down at Freya, and he saw tears of frustration wetting her lashes.

Erik lifted her and grabbed drying cloths as he stepped around the tub to the space before the fire. He lowered her to her feet and rubbed her dry before rushing to the bed to pull a plaid from the foot. He returned and eased Freya to the floor. He settled his body over hers but bore his weight on his forearms.

"I can't," she whimpered again as she clawed at his back and hips. "I need you."

Erik lined his cock up with her entrance.

"Look at me, Freya. Look at me when we become one."

Their blue eyes, different shades of the same color, locked as Erik surged into her. Her back arched off the floor before her arms and legs locked around him. She pulled until his body rested on top of hers. She nudged with her feet until he relented and rested his weight onto her. Freya sighed, and Erik once again felt his cock twitch. Only moments ago, he needed to thrust into her over and over, but now he marveled at how it felt to sink deep within her and not move. Freya ran her hands over his hair and back without much thought as he kissed her neck and earlobes.

"Gods, you are everything to me." Freya confessed, and Erik's heart pinched. He knew such confessions were new to Freya, but he basked in the warmth her openness with him created within his soul. He knew he saw a side of Freya no one else did, and it went far deeper than access to her body.

"The gods brought us together, their wicked sense of humor kept us tormented, but their benevolence joins us. Freya, we are one for eternity."

Declarations made, their bodies rocked against each other with the rhythm they felt when their boats floated into a serene fjord. It was slow and drawn out, allowing them to feel every bit of their bodies' union. When their lips met and tongues danced, it was leisurely. They lavished attention on one another as each sought to heighten the others pleasure, discovering new things their partner enjoyed. The urgency was a slow build until their bodies took control and moved at a pace set by instinct. Their bodies pushed and pulled with increasing speed as their need for release consumed them both. Erik pistoned his rod into Freya as she thrust her hips to meet him time after time. What was only moments ago tender kisses became an aggressive drive to satiate a demand sparked months ago. Freya felt the tautness in her belly grow as her bud became sensitive to the friction they created.

"I'm close, my heart. Just don't stop," she panted. "So close."

Erik felt the spasms begin deep within Freya as they squeezed him. He gritted his teeth and buried his face against the crook of her neck, refusing to climax before her. It was only a moment later that Freya's breath hitched as she cradled Erik's head then moaned. Erik thrust once more before jerking free of her body and spilling onto the linen beneath them. He rolled them so he rested on his back and snatched the blanket to throw it across them. He knew Freya would grow chill since she was still wet. Erik settled her across his chest as they struggled to slow their heart rates. Freya clung to him as though fearful he would set her aside now they were done.

"I'm not going anywhere," he reassured her, but her grip only relaxed a fraction. "Shh," he coaxed her.

Freya's mind could not settle on one emotion. She felt satisfaction and love, but she felt regret and tension knowing Erik pulled out to honor her wishes. She felt unsettled knowing they did not finish together. Somewhere deep inside her, in a way she could not reason through, it felt wrong that they joined to become one and then severed that connection at the moment when they should feel most united. It left her feeling off kilter, and she was not sure how to resolve it.

She lifted her head to look at Erik seeing only love and satisfaction where she felt confusion and unease along with the same feelings he radiated.

"Pennyroyal," she stated.

"What," Erik's brow crinkled.

"Pennyroyal. If I drink a tea made from it, I should be able to keep from conceiving even if you spill your seed within me."

"I don't know about that. Is it safe for you?"

"Women will use it after they conceive," she looked away before looking back with an eyebrow raised, "when they realize they will have a babe they shouldn't."

Erik felt a moment of panic then rage fill him as his mind jumped to a conclusion he dreaded.

"Have you used it," his voice was low and deep as his jaw clenched. The thought she might have conceived Skellig's child took hold.

"No. I've never conceived a child. He never. I never let him." Freya could not finish her thoughts. It felt horrid to discuss her past with the man she loved, was lying across, and had just finished making love to. "Erik, it's well known among women. It's not something spoken about openly, or at least not loudly, but we learn of it when we become old enough to share a bed with a man. I just hadn't thought of it until now. I never had a reason to before."

"Why are you even mentioning it? I can keep pulling out."

"Is that satisfying for you? It isn't for me."

"It's not ideal, but it's safe."

"And ruins it for you."

"Nothing is ruined. It might not feel as good as it did the first time when I didn't pull out. But neither of us is ready to have children. It's only a mere moment during the time when I am joined with you. And that I enjoy more than anything else I could ever feel."

"Maybe. But I feel incomplete somehow. I can't work my way through it, so I don't know how to explain it to you, but somehow I feel cheated by you pulling out. I didn't like ending that closeness before we were done. *Together.* It left me feeling hollow."

Erik kissed her forehead as he cupped her face.

"Can we compromise? Until I can ask my mother, or even Sigrid, if it's safe for you, I will pull out. Once I'm sure it won't endanger you, I will help you find the plant myself."

Freya nodded. She knew it was the most reasonable solution, but she still did not look forward to how their lovemaking would end.

"Does it bother you that much that you no longer want to make love with me? Would you rather wait until we return home?"

Freya's mind railed against that.

"No. Absolutely not. I am not giving this up. When given those choices, I will manage. I'm addicted not only to the physical pleasure, but I crave how our spirits blend into one."

"Those are my feelings too. Freya, I want to see you happy."

"Erik, I am. More so than I have been in ages. I don't know why I feel so maudlin today. But ever since you came close to kissing me in my parents' longhouse the evening we found out about this mission, I haven't looked forward to anything as much as being near you." Freya rested her head over Erik's heart and listened to the steady thump. "I don't care for being an emotional female."

Erik's laughter vibrated below her.

"And you claim I say the most ridiculous things."

They lay there until Erik suggested that she lean over the tub, so they could wash her hair. Then he sat in the lukewarm water only long enough to scrub away the evidence of their travels.

CHAPTER SEVENTEEN

Freya, Erik, and their crew rode with Alex and a small contingent of guardsmen to catch the birlinns back to Alex's home. Alex and his men saw them off before taking their own path back to Varrich. The journey was uneventful, and both Freya and Erik appreciated sailing without responsibility. They stood together at the bow and watched as the coast skimmed past. The wind was with them, so the journey was shorter than they expected. They were back at Castle Varrich before the evening meal. Their reception was not as warm as it had been when Alex was in residence, and Freya suspected his hypothesis about Erik being unavailable had much to do with it. The same woman from their first visit showed them back to their chamber. They knew it would be an early departure, and since Alex would not be present to entertain them, they opted to take their evening meal with their crew in the barracks before retiring early. With regret, they agreed to an early night.

It was still dark when they loaded Freya's longboat with the horses and supplies. It had remained anchored in the natural harbor, so Freya was not concerned for the condition of the boat or whether their bounty was still there. They set sail with the tide and were underway for most of the morning before they saw anything of note. Freund sat in the crow's nest but had not made a peep yet. Freya thought he might have dosed off since he normally called down the most mundane things such as how many birds he could see or the sea creatures he was sure floated below the hull.

"Captain! Ships, Captain! They're making haste with all sails raised."

Freya darted to the stern and placed her spyglass to her eye, facing the direction from which they sailed. Freya could make out the outlines of three ships all with full sails on their mast. There was no mistaking the telltale shape of the Norse longboat. It could only be Grímr or Hakin, or worse, both.

"Hoist the sail and all bodies to the oars," she bellowed. She looked to Erik who watched her. She raised her eyebrows and shrugged. There was nothing they could do to stop their pursuers, but they could put as much distance between them as they could. "I'm banking on his crew not having much experience rowing."

Erik slipped into his spot on his bench as the rowers lowered their oars into the water. His calloused hands did not notice the rub of the wooden handle. Instead he focused on the motions of the oarsman in front of him. He found the synchronized click of the oars soothing as the handles were pressed down to float the flat of the blade over the water before twisting again to drop in at the catch. It was familiar and something to focus on while he was not captaining the boat. He trusted Freya and would not second-guess her, but the distraction eased his nerves when he was not in control.

Freya dashed back to the helm and altered their course to take them beyond the Orkneys and Shetland rather than through the narrow strait they used before. She did not want the landmasses to trap them if Hakin had pirates positioned there. The strait was the more predictable route for boats. She was willing to risk taking the lighter boat in the choppier open water. She trusted her crew, her boat, and herself far more than she worried about the possibility that someone lay in wait.

"Hard on starboard. Port hold water." She directed as she used both the oarsmen and the gusty wind in the sails to change their direction. "As you were." She called once they were on course.

Freya's gaze darted between the outlines of the boats —now visible without the use of the spyglass— and the arcs the rowers' backs made as they swept their blades through the water. She felt as much as saw the shift in current when they reached the open water. She ordered the rowers to pull the oars in until they sailed through the whitecaps that bobbed along where the currents merged. The waves helped to push the boat along, and their progress improved. It appeared they were gaining distance between themselves and the other Norse longboats.

"Captain! To the bow! I see another sail!"

Freya's head whipped up and spotted a boat rounding a small islet in the distance. She knew the crew must have seen them from the other side of the tiny island and maneuvered their way to intercept them.

"Prepare for contact." She had no intention of letting their boats touch unless it was her crew boarding the other boat. First, she needed to see what the crew of the other boat looked like, and that would require getting too close for comfort.

It did not take long before the new ship was making a direct line for Freya's bow. Once again, she ordered the rowers to pull hard to starboard while the port side held their oar blades vertical in the water. It helped whip the bow to port and put them more parallel than perpendicular to the approaching boat. Through the spyglass, she watched as the approaching oarsmen rowed out of synch and ineffectively. It was the motion of the sea and the wind that carried them forward.

"These are not seafarers. They can't get their oars in the water at the same time. We have the advantage there, but I can't see yet how many there are. It looks to be a full crew."

That would mean close to fifty against their less than twenty.

"Freund! Come down and prepare to go to the hull. If I ask, bring the small chest above deck. Make sure it is the smallest one."

Freya was banking on being able to bribe her way out of the ensuing encounter. When they were close enough for Freya to see faces on the other deck, she grinned. While the men were large, most looked green about the gills. They were not accustomed to being on the open seas, and many looked seasick. She looked for whoever was captaining the boat, but it looked as though a crew member was at the tiller.

"Hold water but don't lower the sail all the way. Stand at the ready!" Freya called out.

They floated in place until the other boat came close enough for the crews to call out to one another.

"Prepare to be boarded!" Came a voice from the enemy ship. While strong, it did not match the rest of the crew's appearance.

"By all means, come aboard. We can offer your crew rest and riches," Freya called back.

She watched as several faces turned towards her. Freya was relying on her intuition that she could lure these mercenaries into believing she would out pay both Hakin and Grímr. This would give her the opportunity to gain more thralls and a new boat. Freya just had to tread with caution. She looked at the crew on the other boat and counted to see whether her diminished crew could fight their way through if needed. She spotted the source of the warning and swallowed her gasp. The man was one of the best looking she had ever seen. Only the clasp of a fur cloak covered his broad chest, and he towered over the Highlander mercenaries who were hardly short. He had deep blond hair and flashing ice blue eyes. And he looked remarkably like Erik. She forced herself not to look away when she desperately wanted to find Erik. She wondered if he could see the other Norseman.

Erik stared at a man he had not seen since they were both children. He recognized him in an instant as their family resemblance was uncanny. His cousin always resembled him, but as adults, Erik never knew they were practically twins. His eyes darted to Freya to see her reaction. He watched her take in Tal's appearance and while others might not see it, he registered her shock.

"You must be Freya Ivarsdóttir. The tales told of you don't do you justice," Tal called to her. Erik watched his cousin flash a bright smile at her. It was the same smile Erik used countless times to charm women. He held his breath as he looked to Freya, wondering if it would affect her the way he was sure it did every other woman. She did not look impressed, and he bit back his own grin when he remembered she had plenty of practice ignoring such charm.

"Good thing they don't interest me. You must be Inga and Einar's son." Freya cocked an eyebrow as though her words were not enough of a challenge.

"You have it half right," Tal's tone hardened. "I'm Inga and Grímr's son."

"If you say so." Freya flashed her own grin.

"You've invited me to board you. Shall I come?"

Erik would not remain silent any longer.

"Tal," he called. Erik watched as Tal looked to him, but Freya kept looking straight forward. "It's been a long time, Cousin."

"Erik?"

"Who else would it be? You're quite a way from home. Sailing for your mother or pirating for your uncle?"

Tal sauntered to the rail and grinned now at Erik.

"One and the same, I suppose. Have you been standing there the entire time and didn't invite me aboard your boat? Where are your manners, Cousin? Did that Scots mother of yours forget to teach them?"

Erik smirked, "My wife has already invited you aboard her *boat*, but I shall have to decline your other request."

"Wife is it? I heard our cousin Sigrid married Ivar's son, Leif. Now you've married his daughter. What a cozy family you're all becoming. Such a shame your father keeps choosing the wrong alliances."

Erik saw Tal's small hand gesture just as Freya did and whipped her sword from the scabbard.

"Attack!" Tal bellowed.

"Freund!" Freya yelled in response as her crew scrambled off the benches as sailors from Tal's boat swung grappling hooks and prepared planks to connect their boats. The boy ran awkwardly towards her with the chest.

"Did I not offer you riches?" Freya yelled as she lifted the lid to the chest, and Freund held it up for the enemy to see. "Hakin hired you, but Grímr paid more to make you loyal to him. What if I buy yours with additional riches?"

"Ignore her! What will you each get but a couple of coins? You will receive your reward from Hakin and Grímr when you slay the son and daughter of our enemies."

"But we are not your enemies. We may be your target, but not your enemies." Freya looked at the mercenaries who moved about the deck. They were paying attention to the chest she motioned to. "We could be your employer instead."

Erik saw the greedy stares dart towards the chest, and he prayed Freya calculated the temptation correctly.

"No," Tal spat. "Their loyalty is to Grímr. That is a pittance compared to what my father and uncle offer them."

"Offered but not paid. These riches are here, now, but when will they see what Grímr promised them?" Freya directed her attention to the men who stood on the railing of the boat waiting to jump to hers. "Wouldn't you rather be paid with what you can see and touch than what you may never receive."

"Why wouldn't we just take it?" One toothless man called as he jumped towards Freya's boat. He landed with a thud and an arrow through his neck.

"That is why you would not want to take it." Freya looked at Tal's crew as several more attempted to board her boat and received arrows in their necks and chests. "Would you like to come into our employ or go to your death?"

As one after another was picked off by bow and arrow, the mercenaries appeared to be weighing their options. Freya was sure there were bows and arrows aboard the enemy's boat, but no one pointed them towards her or her crew. Tal was still trying to negotiate with his crew.

"Freya, we're running out of time. Grímr will be on us soon, and then there is no way they will fight for us."

Tal swung across the rails and landed on the deck of Freya's longboat with his sword drawn. He charged towards Erik and Freya.

"You would kill your own blood?" Erik sneered before locking swords with Tal.

Seeing their captain engage was enough to convince the mercenaries to fight rather than accept Freya's offering. She shrugged and whistled to her crew. They were already on their feet with weapons drawn awaiting her signal. The sounds of battle rang out as the mercenaries streamed onto her deck. Freund scrambled back into the crow's nest with a bow and arrow. He picked off man after man as Freya and Erik fought back to back. Tal maintained his onslaught of punishing sweeps and strikes, but Erik's temper was aflame. The betrayal of family against family pulsed through him as his berserker trance took over him. Freya fought one after another as more warriors kept appearing. With their diminished crew, it was a struggle to maintain an upper hand. The deck was becoming slick with blood, and warriors slipped as they tried to wield their weapons to protect themselves and kill their opponents.

Erik's vision tunneled with the edges faded to black as he focused on Tal. They played together as children when Inga came for visits, but there had always been a spiteful nature Tal did little to hide back then or now. He hissed insults about Erik's mother, Lorna, and described what he would do to Freya the moment he killed Erik. Erik heard little of what his cousin said. The blood pounded in his ears as he swung his sword over and over. He struggled to keep his footing as blood and surf splashed around his boots. He kept his back to Freya intuitively aware of her even when he saw nothing more than his foe. Tal lunged exposing his entire right side. Erik struck hard and fast, slashing his sword through Tal's ribs. The man dropped to his knees as blood squirted from his flank. He tried to cover the wound with his hand, but the blood still gushed.

"You won't die from that, but you will be in fucking agony."

"Erik!" Freya nudged him before pointing across the stern. "You were right. We shall have company soon."

"Get the survivors into the hull and the dead over the side. I'll take Tal's boat and the remaining crew who don't want to die."

Freya and Erik moved to get both Freya's boat and Erik's newly acquired one under way. Tal lay on the deck where Erik left him. He did not have the strength to move and posed little threat except from his venomous tongue.

"Those are my father's boats approaching. You may have been able to defeat one with shite for a crew, but my father's is filled with proper Norse warriors and sailors. You may as well surrender now."

"Like you did? For a dying man, you talk a lot. I would save the air for when your lungs fill with blood, and you're suffocating."

Freya watched as her crew led the injured attackers to the hull to lock them into the large cage built to hold captives. They forced those in good enough shape onto benches to row. The crew dumped the rest over the side for the sea god to bury. Erik's men accompanied him onto Tal's boat to sail that one.

"My father will take no mercy on you. You will find yourself bent over the side while he takes you in front of your entire crew, and your weak husband has no choice but to watch his pretty little wife take another man's cock."

Freya walked on silent feet to him and stood looking down. Her face was expressionless, so Tal was unprepared for when her booted foot struck out and landed near his gaping wound.

"Your father isn't bending anyone over anything. He's dead. Einar is dead, and we all know he was your father. You are little more than a bastard Grímr toys with promising an inheritance he will never have to give. Your mother is a whore who cuckolded Grímr for years. Now he is half lame with a hatred that burns hotter for Hakin and Inga than it does anyone else. Let Grímr come for us. Do you have any idea where that chest came from? The one my barrelman held. We raided your mother's farm."

Freya watched as surprise flickered across his face.

"That's right. We took it all. And we let the women go. There is nothing left for Grímr or Hakin to pay anyone with. And your whoring mother has no one left to sell. You have no homestead left to go to either. You will die on this boat without a sword in your hand. So, let Grímr come. Let Hakin come. They can die just as you will. With nothing."

Freya gave him another kick for good measure before returning to the helm. She noticed a commotion coming from Erik's boat. Freya looked over to see a woman pulled from under a bench. The older woman looked a great deal like Erik but was almost the spitting image Sigrid, her sister-in-law and Erik's cousin.

Can this get any more twisted? That must be Inga. I guess Sigrid's mother must have looked a great deal like Inga rather than like Erik's father.

"Tangled family tree, isn't it? Eerie how much we all look alike." Tal tried to laugh but it came out more as a splutter. "My mother and her sister were two sides of the same coin. That's why Sigrid looks so much like my mother. My Uncle Rangvald would look much like his sisters if he didn't have the beard. Erik took after his father's side rather than his Highlander mother's."

"How convenient for your mother that you all look so much alike. It must have made keeping her secrets much easier."

Freya moved away from the helm to get a better look. The woman was as beautiful as Sigrid, with platinum blond hair and dark blue eyes. Her features were proportionate and soft, but the look in her eyes was as hard as chiseled marble. They shot sparks of hatred at her and at Erik. Her lip curled in disgust as she looked at Freya.

"I heard you say you've stolen from me." Her high-pitched voice grated across Freya's nerves.

"No more than your lover, husband, and brother-in-law turned lover have done to us." Freya crossed her arms and smirked. There was something evil about the woman that sent ripples of fear through Freya, but she would never let it show. She watched the woman's back straighten as her chin snapped up.

"Taunt me all you want, little girl, but I have played this game far longer than you have been alive."

"Maybe so, but let's not forget that I'm alive because my father sent you back and married my mother. The woman he loves. And wants."

Freya gripped her sleeves within her crossed arms, forcing herself to still her tongue. She could not let herself get drawn into a catfight with Erik's aunt. They needed to sail from their pursuers. Ones she forgot temporarily while facing the present danger.

"Freya, we shall hold her for ransom if Grímr catches us. Assuming he even wants her. If not, we turn her over to my father." Erik yanked Inga to the center mast and tied her to the post. "Speak again, Aunt Inga, and I shall tie you to the prow. You can pray you don't drown."

CHAPTER EIGHTEEN

Both crews moved with haste once they secured and stowed all captives. Erik's crew went to the oars along with the remaining mercenaries. Many of them were still puce, but a drive to stay alive gave them the energy they did not muster during the battle. One of Erik's men found a whip and stood ready to crack it against the back of any man who could not keep up. Freya's crew took up their oars. The two women, Helga and Alva, were her two steadiest and reliable pacers, so they sat as stroke on the port and starboard sides. Freya's crew were used to the wicked pace both women could keep and followed their lead pushing the longboat further into open water. The sail caught a gust and jumped with the bow slamming hard as the bottom dropped out from the wave it rode. The boat bobbed around like a child's toy swirling around a drain, but Freya knew it would hold. This was not the first challenging course she charted. She considered what Tyra would tell her. She pictured her friend at the tiller of her own boat, more sea goddess than mortal, always at one with the ocean. Erik's new longboat fell in just to the right of hers. He called his own instructions to his crew as their boats raced to put a safer distance between them and their pursuers. They lost valuable time allowing the other Norsemen to gain on them. Freya looked back over her shoulder and nodded to Erik before looking at the three boats cutting through the whitecaps. They were larger boats with larger sails and more rowers, but Freya was relying on their lighter boats sitting higher in the water and moving faster.

Erik's eyes scanned the horizon while he knew Freya was watching their sterns. He caught sight of Orkney and knew they still had all the daylight hours and several into the night before they would pass Shetland. It would be two more days before they would reach the coast of their homeland. He shook his head. They could not get there soon enough.

"Erik," Freya's voice carried on the wind. "We can outrun them as long as the wind holds, but if it dies, we shall be nothing more than sitting targets for them. Do we sail for Shetland and try to lose them among the islets and islands? I can think of several coves, but I don't know if they know of them. They will either give us shelter or trap us."

"Let's carry on as we are. Once night falls, we will have to decide. The best we can pray for is a heavy cloud cover."

Freya and Erik looked towards the horizon and saw nothing but clear open blue skies with no clouds visible.

The crew rowed whenever the wind died down and rested when gusts pushed them along. Freund called his estimates any time they seemed to slacken or gain distance between them and their enemies. Neither Inga nor Tal would say whether it was just Grímr or if Hakin was there too. They remained far enough apart that even with the spyglass, Freya could not see faces or even make out the carvings on the prow. She counted that as a small blessing.

The sun faded and with it the wind calmed. Freya swore up a storm in her mind as her exhausted crew once again dropped their oars into the water. Sweat drenched Helga and Alva, but the two women maintained a fierce pace only the most experienced of rowers could keep. Freya ended up ordering the mercenaries away from the oars since they could not keep up and their blades clashed with her experienced crew. She put most to work cleaning the blood from the deck, and one tended to Tal. Freund remained in the crow's nest with his bow and arrow poised in case any of the new thralls attempted mutiny.

Erik kept an eye on Freya as he captained his own boat. He tried to block out the constant nagging and prattling of his aunt Inga. It was almost dark, and the temperature plummeted when he handed off the tiller to his first mate. Erik walked to his aunt. Without a word, he unbound her arms, but before she could do anything to rub feeling back into them, he yanked her elbow and moved towards the bow. He re-tied her hands and looped a long rope through the binding around her wrists.

"Step up, Aunt Inga."

"I'll do no such thing."

"I warned you, and you tested me. Now you have failed. I'm tying you to the dragonhead."

"You can't do that. You wouldn't dare. I'm still your father's sister. I demand to see my son."

"You forfeited that the moment you betrayed us. We know now that was years ago. I have no forgiveness for you, and I won't show you any mercy. Your son can rot on the deck of my wife's boat for all I could care." Erik yanked her again until he could push her to the large carved dragon head. He nudged her until she stepped onto the figurehead that jutted out over the water.

"Lie down," Erik ordered.

Inga tried to fight him, but he sank his hands into her hair and clutched a fistful. He held her head in place.

"Don't make this worse. I feel no guilt contemplating killing you. Don't push me to it. This way you might survive. Anger me and there is no chance of that."

Inga inched out and lay flat with her arms stretched over her head. Erik made quick work of wrapping the rope around her middle and then cinching it tight around her ankles to keep her fastened to the dragon figure.

"You will pay for this."

"I doubt it."

The wind swallowed anything Inga uttered.

"What say you?" Erik called to Freya as he stepped to the rail.

Freya handed over the wheel to her own first mate and stood across from Erik. She looked at the smudges trailing them. They could barely see the boats, but Erik and Freya knew they were still there.

"We should be nearing Shetland's southern isles within the hour. I think we use the dark to change course and swing into the sound near Brusey. They'll think we went for the Isle of Noss because it's shorter, but then we can follow behind them. They'll have no idea whether we sail straight across the open water to Stjordal or followed the coast."

"And which do you suggest we do? Open water or coast?"

"Let's see how much distance we put between us. Obviously, open water would be faster, but the coast offers plenty of places to hide."

"And plenty of places to be found."

"True. Whether by them or someone else. Either way, we should still be home in less than two days."

"Then we battle, and after that, I shall bed my wife the right way."

"I shall hold you to that."

"I can think of exactly what I want you to hold." Erik's teeth shone in the dark. It was the only feature Freya could discern, and it made her think of the things his mouth could do to her.

"And I can think of exactly where I want to hold it." Erik's chuckle floated to her, and she felt warmed despite the drop in temperature as they sailed further north.

There was nothing more to say, and they both knew they needed to return to the tillers. Freya turned away but paused.

"There isn't anyone I rely on as I do you. There is no one else I'd want to rely on as I do you. Not Bjorn or Strian, not even Leif or Tyra."

"I was thinking the same thing, my love. I trust you without thought and rely on you without worry."

"We make a good team."

"We do. On water and even better in bed."

Freya's peal of laughter hung in the air as she went to relieve her first mate. Fatigue settled over everyone, but the risk of death or worse, being made a thrall, kept them all moving. Freya guided the two boats as they shifted to the east. She checked her maps and star charts to guide her into the channel between Brusey and the Shetland mainland. They would travel through until they could enter the North Sea. If Grímr or Hakin followed them, the waterway was wide enough not to trap them, but she asked the gods to favor her luck with safe passage. Their boats cruised past the south tip of the island, and she guided them close to the coast in the hopes the shadows of the landmass would help hide them. Everyone aboard the boats was silent, with both Erik and Freya ordering their crews to pull their oars in for the first quarter of an hour they were in the sound.

Then Freya dared call up to Freund for a report. She listened to the sleepy voice drift down to her with a report that he could see nothing following them. The wind caught between the two landmasses bounced from shore to shore and billowed their sails, moving them faster and with greater ease than any rowers could. It only took another quarter hour before they were at the head of the channel. They lowered the sails to wait out the night. Freya breathed a sigh of relief as she handed out rations to her crew and assigned them shifts to sleep. She looked over at Tal and could see the shallow rise and fall of his chest. She wished he would slip away rather than linger as a burden. Freya tossed the stalest piece of bread she had at him. He grunted as he reached a bloody hand out and snatched it up.

Freya nor Erik could not see each other, but they could each see the bulk of the other ship as they bobbed near the shore until the sun's early rays touched the eastern horizon. As the sun pinkened, Erik's and Freya's longboats inched into the North Sea. There was nothing and no one to see for miles. Erik kept looking around as discomfort hovered over him and raised the hair on the back of his neck. Something did not feel right. It was too easy.

He used his spyglass to look back at the Isle of Noss as they once again entered open water. The water was calm that morning, but he knew it was as deceptive as Loki. The varying depths and shifting currents made sailing choppy, and storms generated out of what appeared to be nothing. Erik tried to reassure himself that it was the unnatural calm water that made him uneasy and not the uncertainty of whether their pursuers passed them in the night.

Freya felt her own unease as she set a course to cross the open water and make the most direct line to Stjordal and her home.

"Freund! What see you?"

"Nothing, Captain. Not even a bird."

Freya remembered what Tyra warned her before they left. No birds were a warning. She pulled out her spyglass and scanned the sky in every direction trying to catch a glance of where the storm might brew. She could see nothing, but the longer they sailed northeast, the more she was sure she could smell an approaching gale.

Erik strode to the prow and checked on his aunt. She shivered and was damp, but still alive. He wondered if he regretted her being alive as much as Freya regretted Tal surviving. Erik had seen her kick him the night before and had to bite his lip to keep from smiling. He did not feel mercy as a natural emotion during battle, but he had wondered if he could conjure some for his family members. He could not. Erik felt no guilt treating them the same as any prisoner, and he would not offer either of them comforts or afford them any privileges. He shook Inga's foot.

"Wake if you slept," he barked as he untied her from the prow.

She slid gracelessly to the deck and huddled in a soggy mass of tangled hair and limbs. She raised her eyes to shoot daggers at him, but Erik was already tugging her to her feet.

"Save your hate for someone who cares enough to notice."

Inga stumbled as her frozen limbs screamed when blood rushed into them and she expected them to move. Erik dumped her next to the mast, called for a fur, and after she wrapped it around herself, he tied her to the mast again.

"Stay quiet or back you go," he warned.

Inga prudently kept quiet, but her mutinous glare did not abate. Erik shook his head as he crossed the deck and retook the wheel.

Erik kept his boat's bow just even with the bow of Freya's boat. They nodded to one another once in a while, but there was little to say, so they focused on their crews and navigating the growing whitecaps. It was midday when the storm materialized and dumped on them. As though being chased and having to hide was not enough, now the gods thought to laugh at them by sending a storm. Thor's war cry rattled the planks of their boats as lightning streaked across the sky. They were little more than weathervanes bouncing along a massive electrical conductor. The torrential rain hammered down on them with both crews forced to bail. Erik and Freya risked their sails, but they kept them hoisted, taking advantage of the gale-force winds to push them along and past the storm. The wind and rain raged the rest of the day and through the night.

Freya swore she would not step on another boat for at least a year if they made it home in one piece. She shivered over and over as she stood lashed to the tiller. The two crews tied themselves to the benches or the mast of their boats to keep from being swept overboard. The night seemed to last forever, but as the sun rose on their third day at sea, the rain ended with the same abruptness as it started. Within minutes of the last drop, they heard the screeches of seagulls.

"At least that means the storm didn't blow us off course," Erik observed as they came to stand across from one another. "Where do you estimate we are?"

"I don't know yet. I haven't seen any landmarks I can make out on any of the maps, but I would venture a guess at being north of Giske."

"Then we still have a day of sailing left."

"Yes. The wind helped in some ways, but the waves slowed us too."

"Freya, we can't rely on the wind and current. We will have them row. I hate saying this, but we need to cast this one adrift and combine the crew again. They need rest and shifts. If we encounter Hakin or Grímr, we will need double the rowers to flee or to fight. Though fighting is hardly ideal with this lot. They have no allegiance to us and are likely to switch sides as easily as they did before. Your boat is lighter than this one even if smaller. It'll make better time."

"Set the grappling hooks and bring them all aboard."

Freya readied her boat by having all the port oarsman once again drop their oar blades vertically into the water to hold their forward progress. Erik and his loyal crew ferried the others across then they ransacked the storage beneath the deck boards. They brought anything they could toss or pass over before boarding too. Erik pulled Inga along and deposited her next to Tal who was pale and clammy. A nasty fever set in during the storm. Inga screamed and wrapped her son into her arms. She sat huddled with him as she sobbed.

"Your tears are wasted. He's too close to dead to appreciate them, and none of us care." Freya sneered. Inga sat rocking with Tal's head nestled in her lap.

"You're soaked. You should get changed, Freya."

Freya stepped into Erik's open arms. It had only been a day since they stood together, but it felt like an eternity after weathering both a battle and a storm, not to mention the chase.

"You are too. Come to the cabin. The others are taking their turns going to the hold to change."

They walked to Freya's cabin and once inside peeled out of their wet clothes. Erik pulled out two drying cloths and rubbed Freya's arms and back. She moaned as the blood rushed through her chilled flesh. She ran the linen over Erik's chest and abdomen.

"I can think of much more effective way to warm up," she murmured as she watched his rod surge to life.

Erik trailed his fingers from her collarbones to her nipples and when she shivered with pleasure rather than cold, he lowered his mouth to hers. Their kiss was languid while their hands explored one another. Erik slid his to her bottom and pressed her against the hard planes of his body. Her arms snaked around his neck as she tipped her head back giving him the access to her throat he sought. His tongue savored the salty taste of the skin exposed to the elements and then the honey sweet nipples. He flicked one then tugged the other with his teeth.

"How can you still taste like honey? How is that even possible? I'm sure you haven't bathed with it since we left your home."

Freya shrugged.

"I've been doing it for years. It takes months before it wears off. It's been a fortnight."

"I intend to slather you with honey and lick ever drop from you as soon as we are home."

"I don't need honey to want to lick you."

Erik pinched her bottom as they sank into another kiss. However, a pounding on the door interrupted them.

"Captain," Freund's young voice came through the closed door. "They've spotted us."

"Of course," Freya muttered. "I should have known we wouldn't have any time."

She pulled clothes from her trunk as Erik pulled clothes from his own chest. They dressed and dashed back to the helm. Several leagues to the west were three boats making a direct line for them.

"The storm blew them off course," Erik surmised. "We can get ahead of them again, but only if we have every able body at the oars. I'll take care of that while you navigate."

He strode back to his bench barking orders as he went. Helga and Alva settled back into their spots and began their count and calls. The experienced oarsmen partnered with the less-experienced rowers to guide their rhythm and direct their form. Gautri paced the center aisle, whip in hand, prepared to crack it across the back of any thrall not doing his share. The mercenaries saw the instrument of discipline and understood their demoted status from warrior to slave. None seemed interested in being on the receiving end of the leather strap.

"Back into the nest, Freund." The boy scampered past her and clambered up the mast.

"Captain, they're down to two boats!" Freund hooted.

"Are you sure? One isn't sailing in another's wake?"

"Nope. I have a clear view. There are only two there. I can't see anything else anywhere."

"Perhaps one floundered in the storm."

Freya wanted to feel relieved, but she knew that would only tempt fate, and fate was already taunting them enough. She did not need to make it worse. Three hours later, the oarsmen were flagging as the sun beat down on them. Freund gave regular reports, and the distance remained great enough that Freya called a rest. She allowed the crew a half hour of rest before Erik rotated them through shifts. They made steady progress with no more interference, and Freya wanted to squeal in excitement when she recognized the shoreline as the sun dropped below the horizon. They were only a few hours from home. If they could stay ahead of the enemy boats, they would sail into her homestead's fjord without being intercepted. She wished there was a way to warn her family though. Instead, she would bring the enemy straight to their door.

CHAPTER NINETEEN

It was the dead of night when she blew the horn to announce their arrival. The sound echoed through the silence and rang against the cliffs as they approached the docks of her home. She continued to blow the horn until she heard one in return that she was sure was not just an echo. Freya and Erik stood together watching the light from torches jog towards the dock. The entire tribe, along with Erik's family and their warriors, poured down the hill to greet them.

"There's my father," Erik's hushed tones held a note of worry. Freya looked at him, but he was looking at Inga and Tal. Tal had not survived and lay dead beside his mother's prostrate body. She ceased making any sound several hours earlier.

"They are the only ones to blame for their fate."

"I know, but I can't imagine what my father will think when he sees his sister and hears what she's done." Erik shook his head as his mouth turned down in a deep frown.

Freya reached out and smoothed the skin between his brows, then took his hand until they sailed alongside the dock.

"Daughter!" Ivar exclaimed as he led the entourage to greet them. Beside him were Freya's mother Lena and Erik's parents, Rangvald and Lorna. Leif and Sigrid followed, with Erik's brothers and sisters jostling in front of Strian, Bjorn, and Tyra.

"Father!" Erik and Freya called as one.

The crew tied the boat and prepared to disembark. Freya and Erik hung back. They let their crew reunite with their families while giving their own pointed looks that told their families not to ask questions yet. Lorna sent her other children back to the homestead to assist with preparing a proper welcome home. Erik pulled Inga to her feet and handed her off to Freya before lifting Tal into his arms.

Rangvald pushed forward and caught his sister as Freya practically flung her from the boat.

"Inga?" Rangvald murmured, stunned at his sister's appearance.

"Fuck you and your family," she spat.

Rangvald drew his arm back, but Lorna was faster. Her fist smashed into the other woman's face.

"What have you done, Inga?" Rangvald demanded.

"Your son and his whore killed my son." Rangvald looked over Inga's head as Erik leapt to the dock with Tal still in his arms.

"He got himself killed by attacking us. It's not our fault he attacked at sea where there was no way to put ashore and tend him." He scowled at Inga before muttering, "Not that we would have."

"What in Odin's name happened? You were only supposed to scout," Ivar broke in. He glued his eyes to the way Freya stood with her arm around Erik's waist.

"A great deal of things, Father. I can explain all after we retire to our chamber long enough to get cleaned up. I have three-day-old blood on me still."

"Daughter, what in the gods' name do you mean by 'chamber?' Why was that not plural?"

"Because I married your daughter." Erik shifted Tal in his arms and stepped forward. Freya and the others followed him until he deposited the body at the end of the dock. "We have thralls in the hold, and Inga needs locking up."

Freya slid her hand into his and led them back to the family's longhouse. When the entire group reached the main room, Erik and Freya turned towards her chamber.

"Hold on. What do you mean you're married? I thought you'd be wiser than your brother." Ivar huffed.

"I was. I didn't make him run away. He chased me."

"Wait a moment now," Leif piped in, but Sigrid nudged him.

"Jarl Ivar, we pledged ourselves as Leif and Sigrid did without a sacrifice, but I called upon my mother's heritage and consider us wed through a handfast." Erik anchored Freya to his side, daring anyone to disagree or try to separate them.

Ivar and Lena exchanged the same look Rangvald and Lorna exchanged. Both sets of parents shrugged.

"That's it?" Leif demanded.

"Of course, it is. We knew this was inevitable. Half the reason we sent them off together was to move things along. Neither were happy, him chasing her and her running from him." Lorna stepped forward to embrace Freya. "Welcome to the family. Finally. About bluidy time. No more dithering about."

Lorna winked at Freya before asking none too quietly, "Do ye think a bairn is on the way yet?"

Freya flushed a deep red, and Erik pulled his wife loose from his mother. He scooped Freya into his arms and strode to her chamber.

"I will have your belongings moved here at once."

Erik kicked the door shut and moved before the fire. The thralls moved with haste. There was already a steaming tub set on the hearth.

"I'm glad this is here. I was not looking forward to sharing the bathhouse with the other men. I wanted to bathe with you."

"You do owe me the chance to make love in water." Freya was already stripping and flinging her clothes into a pile.

Erik matched her urgency as he peeled his tunic and leather pants off. He lifted her off her feet, and her legs came around his waist as he slid into her. Their mouths devoured one another as Erik moved to the tub. He pulled his lips free long enough to ensure he could step in without dropping her. They sank into the hot water as their tongues once again tangled. Erik ran his hands over her hair and along her back until he cupped her backside. The water swished around their bodies as they rocked together. Neither could think of anything to say, instead resting their foreheads against one another as they looked into each other's eyes. As the pleasure crept from her core into her chest and through her limbs, Freya tilted her head back letting her eyelids drift closed. Erik sprinkled kisses across her chest while her fingers knitted into his hair and her nails grazed his scalp.

A loud knock sounded at the door snapping Freya out of the trance Erik's touch created. She looked around and spotted two bars of soap on the table beside the tub. She picked up one and hurled it at the door. It crashed against the wood and fractured into shards as she hollered, "Go away."

Silence greeted their ears. Whoever it was thought better than interrupting again.

"We haven't long, my heart," Freya whispered. "I know we can't hide here. Not yet at least."

"I'm not letting you go anywhere until I hear you shriek my name to the heavens."

Freya cupped his jaw in her hands and fell upon his mouth as they pawed each other. Need overcame the desire to linger. Erik gripped her hips as he thrust his into hers. Needing to ground herself, Freya grabbed the lip of the tub behind Erik's back. Their moans filled the room blending with the slosh of the water and the crackle of the fire.

"Erik!" Freya's scream filled the room but was cut off with Erik's responding, "Freya!"

Erik lifted her from him before spilling his seed. Freya dropped her head to Erik's shoulder feeling boneless and exhausted. He leaned back as his heart continued to race.

"I'm getting that damn pennyroyal tonight," Freya panted.

Another, more insistent, knock came at the door.

"Just wait," Erik called. "We'll be there."

Once again, whoever stood on the other side chose wisely to retreat. The couple made short work of scrubbing one another, and Erik washed Freya's hair just as he had at Castle Varrich.

"I have no clothes to put on."

"Check outside the door. It wouldn't surprise me if a thrall was trying to deliver them." Freya's estimation was correct, and Erik found two of his chests outside the door. With only a drying cloth wrapped around his hips, he brought both trunks inside. Freya pointed out a space next to hers. She beamed as she looked at what appeared to be a matching set.

"Do you like the look of them? Are my belongings and I to be treasures you display?"

"Definitely not. You are not for anyone to look at in this chamber but me. No letting the thralls see you in the bare, Erik. I won't take that well."

"I have no desire for anyone to see me naked but you. There is no reason for any other woman to see me without a stitch on." Erik frowned as a thought crossed his mind. "I don't like the men seeing you when we travel, and you have to bathe at a river."

"They don't," Freya's brow crinkled. "Do they?"

"I caught more than a passing glance many times. I'm sure others could see what I did. I did what I could to keep them away, so I wouldn't explode.

But before that," Erik shrugged. "I can only imagine what they saw of you and Tyra."

Freya blushed as she stepped to Erik and ran her hands over his chest.

"We only see each other naked, agreed?"

"Absolutely," he pecked her nose and they finished dressing.

Erik and Freya could smell food wafting towards them from the unplanned midnight feast. They walked into the main hall hand-in-hand and garnered more than a few stares. Erik spotted Skellig scowling in the corner, but the man did not move. Erik hoped Ivar's henchman had ended Skellig's plans because he was not looking forward to dealing with him, but he would end Skellig's belief he had a claim on Freya. If it meant running him through, Erik had not a flicker of regret. The couple walked to the jarl's table and found someone rearranged the seating for them to sit together. Both their mothers beamed with satisfaction as Rangvald and Ivar stood to greet them.

Rangvald pulled his son into a close embrace and slapped him on the back hard enough for several bones to pop.

"Do anything to take that smile from her face, and I will punish you personally," his voice for Erik's ears only.

"Father, you don't have to worry. I love Freya as much as you love Mother."

Rangvald nodded before teasingly pushing him away in favor of Freya who he hugged with more care.

"I could not ask for a better woman to join our tribe or wife for my son. I'm blessed with two beautiful daughters and now the gods have granted me another."

Freya found Rangvald's embrace as soothing as her father's, and she let herself nestle into him and the fur cloak draped over his chest. Erik shook hands with Ivar before receiving another bone cracking embrace.

"I'll kill you if you make my daughter unhappy," Ivar's voice was not as hushed as Rangvald's.

"And who is to defend me if she makes me cry?" Erik teased. Erik looked around at the smiling faces, but no one did more than shrug.

"Worry not, husband. I'm sure I can soothe those tears." Freya tapped him on the backside before Erik pulled her in for a searing kiss that had both jarls clearing their throats and people banging their tankards on the table.

"We better see to the preparations for tomorrow's ceremony and festivities," Lena spoke over the din as she looked to Lorna.

"Mama, no. I don't want a big deal made of the ceremony. Let there be a feast for everyone to enjoy, but I don't need anything more."

"You need to go through the same rituals as Sigrid did," Lorna smiled.

Freya shook her head.

"No, if I have to go through those, then Erik has to do what Leif did. I'm not making my husband go digging around a burial ground for what may not be there. We're marrying away from his home. His father won't have a sword here for him. I won't have him searching through catacombs for something that doesn't exist."

"That is where you are mistaken," Rangvald interjected. "It was obvious the moment the two of you met that there were sparks. By the time we chased after you and Sigrid back to my homestead, we all knew you and Erik would marry. You were half in love by then. I slipped my father's sword in with the rest of our belongings. Lorna already knew we would need it."

Rangvald beamed at his wife. Freya was not sure if he was proud of his wife's forethought or proud that he listened.

"So, there is no escaping the ritual preparations?"

"Nope," Leif spoke up as he helped Sigrid to her chair. She was showing a noticeably rounded belly now, and Freya could not keep from smiling as she thought about a niece or nephew to spoil. She had a moment of regret that there was little chance she could be carrying. As Erik's grip tightened around her, she rested her head against his shoulder.

"Whenever you are ready, but not a moment sooner," he whispered.

"I love you," she mouthed.

"I love you, too."

Freya and Erik took turns recounting the events of their mission. They shared the information they discovered on Orkney and in the Highlands. They told of the ambush and the pursuit. Erik and Freya warned that Hakin and Grímr would find Tal's boat cast adrift. They estimated Hakin and Grímr would arrive by morning considering how closely they tailed them. Everyone agreed neither Hakin nor Grímr would attempt another night attack from the sea. They would wait until they had daylight to guide them.

The conversation moved on, and the meal proceeded without incident, but Erik kept an eye on the crowd to see if anyone else might be less than joyous at their union. He watched several women flutter their eyes at him, but he felt nothing at the overtures. He was more interested in the men and their reaction to Freya no longer being available. A few looked with appreciation at her. Until they realized Erik saw them. They ducked their heads or looked away. Even Skellig seemed intent on seducing the woman now seated on his lap.

"If another one bats her eyelashes at you, we shall have a homestead of blind women," Freya grumbled.

"And a homestead of toothless men if they don't stop leering at you."

Erik wove his fingers between hers and kissed the back of her hand.

Freya looked at the food being cleared away and felt a consuming need to escape. There were too many people with too many eyes and ears. She wanted time alone with her husband. She wanted to fall asleep in his arms, sleep like the dead until sunrise, and then wake basking in the warmth of his body next to hers. "Can we go now? Erik, please. I don't want to stay any longer."

Erik looked down surprised by the sudden shift in Freya. He felt waves of tension radiate from her stiff body.

"What's wrong?" he kept his voice for only her to hear.

"It's too much. Too many people. Too much noise. I'm exhausted, and I only want to be with you."

Erik stood from his spot on the bench and helped Freya to her feet. Other members of the family saw Freya's exhausted features and their mothers nodded. It was Rangvald who shook his head.

"I'm sorry, Erik, but I need you to come with me to interrogate Inga. It won't take long, and if it seems like it will, I'll send you to Freya."

Freya swallowed the lump rising in her throat. She was never this emotional before she admitted her feelings for Erik. She wondered if she would be too weak to be a warrior now. The couple left the main chamber, and Erik escorted Freya to their chamber.

"I'll stay. There's no reason my father can't speak to Inga without me. I think he wants me there to keep him from throttling her."

"No. You'll be a jarl one day, and I'll be your *frú*. We both have duties that go before what we want. I shall be fine. I'm just tired after months on the water and in battle. I need some quiet."

"Freya, I don't want to leave you."

"Erik," exasperation filled her tone. "I don't need coddling. I just need some damn quiet. I'm not weak just bloody tired."

Erik stood to his full height as he looked at his wife.

"I never thought you were weak. Did it not occur to you that maybe *I* need *you*? Did you ever think perhaps *I* want the comfort of my wife rather than another round of battle?"

Freya slid her hands up his chest and placed both over his heart.

"You shall never cease to amaze me. Part of me hates knowing you ever feel vulnerable. It doesn't fit with how I think of you. But another part of me is awed by your willingness to show that side to me. It makes me know I'm not alone in my feelings."

They kissed each other's cheeks, nipped at each other's jaws, and at last, their lips brushed together not once but thrice before melding together. Freya tasted of the sweet mead served with the meal. It only took two swipes of his tongue, and Erik felt intoxicated. Freya clung to him to keep her legs from buckling. She mimicked the motion she intended to lavish upon him later that night. She could feel his steel sword pressing against her sheath as his arms encircled her waist and pinned her lithe form against his.

"You are temptation incarnate, wife. How will I ever get anything done when I never want to leave our chamber again?"

"I want to beg you to stay, but it will only draw out my agony. Hurry, so you can be back sooner." Freya pulled away and wrapped her arms around her middle.

"I'll return as soon as I can. I promise." Erik was determined not to look back, but when he got to the door, he could not stop himself. Freya waved to him, and he nodded before slipping into the corridor.

CHAPTER TWENTY

Freya undressed and slipped into a light linen tunic she knew was transparent when she stood before the fire. She pulled a fur around her as she sat watching the flames dance. She let herself doze in the hopes it would make the time pass faster.

Erik found his father, Ivar, and Leif outside the longhouse. Leif looked sympathetic, but the two fathers looked smug.

"Welcome to the club, Son. I hate leaving your mother more than anything else. There are many days I would trade being jarl for a moment longer in her arms."

Ivar led the way to the building that held prisoners and thralls convicted of crimes. It was more of a three-walled shelter with a wall of bars and a *níðstöng*, or scorn-pole, erected in the center. The three walls and roof sheltered the scorned person from the elements, but anyone passing by could see whomever they tied to it. The four men approached and heard Inga before they saw her. The woman's ranting rattled off the walls as she spewed venom cursing everyone she could think of.

"Silence, woman," Rangvald barked. "Your actions shame our family, but your deranged rantings will make the gods question your place in the afterlife."

"What do I care of the afterlife? You've taken my lover and my son from me. What have I left?"

"I don't know. Perhaps your husband and other children?" Leif threw at her.

Ivar shot him a quelling look, but Leif said what all four men thought.

Inga laughed and the cackle bordered on hysteria. She shook her head.

"That milksop. He knows my children aren't his. Einar kept me pregnant too often for Grímr's seed to ever take."

Ivar grimaced and shot Leif a look of disgust. It had been difficult for Ivar to accept that his most trusted warrior not only murdered Ivar's former second in command, who happened to be the man's brother, but he had coveted Lena. His covetousness led him to betray them all by selling himself and the tribe's secrets to Hakin. Leif shook his head as pity crossed his face. The pity was not for the woman before him but the worst betrayal of all. Einar had been his friend Strian's uncle. The man murdered his wife and left their children as orphans and Strian with no family left. The man's selfishness left a trail of victims, the least of which was the crazy woman held in the cell before them.

"Why, Inga? What did I do to deserve this," Rangvald's hushed tones betrayed his anguish. "I brought you home when Father made a match that would make you miserable. I tried to make a match that would make you happy. A man who loved you and a comfortable home. Why turn on us? Was it Einar's wish? Grímr's or Hakin's? Or did you do this on your own?"

"You have no idea, do you?" Inga's cackle reverberated in the small building. "You took away my opportunity to be *frú* by marrying me to a second son. Worthless man. I was meant to be the wife of a jarl. It just wasn't meant to be with this man whose balls are held by the woman he whored with while married to me."

Ivar reached through the bars, but Inga was quicker and danced out of the way.

"Don't speak of Lena that way. I never wanted you whether or not I loved Lena. I saw this side to you and wanted nothing to do with it. I was lucky enough to already love the woman the gods meant me to have. Ours was no real marriage. It was but a trial, and everyone knows it. Our foolish fathers willed it, but thank the gods, I wasn't stuck with your viperous tongue."

Inga's eyes shot sparks of hatred at Ivar. There had been no love lost between them, but Inga's ambition suffered when Rangvald and Sigrid's mother, Signy, brought her home. It had been only two moons later that their father was dead and Rangvald was jarl. It was another two moons before Grímr married Inga. Somewhere in that time, she fell in love with Einar.

"Who seduced who?" Rangvald asked.

"I seduced Einar, but I was his and he was mine. Never mind our legal families. Neither of us wanted them. The only one who mattered was Tal. And now he is gone. He would have been the greatest jarl to ever rule the Trondelag."

Erik let his laughter rumble to the surface. He looked at his aunt and curled his lip as though he smelled something repugnant.

"He was inept. When we were children and when he attacked. He was impetuous and driven by ego. Now he's dead."

Inga wailed and yanked at her hair with both hands. Rangvald shot his son a censorious glare, and Erik tilted his head in deference.

"Inga, I still don't understand. Why? You weren't at the homestead when Leif and his crew raided it. Where were you?"

"I had a farm on Orkney. It was a good location to do business. I was there."

"Business?" Rangvald asked.

"Father, she took the women of marriageable age from her tribe and sold them to the mercenaries as part of their payment. Those she didn't promise to the men she planned to sell to the east."

Rangvald staggered back and covered his heart with his fist. He rubbed the weight that settled there.

"You would betray your own people? You would sell your own women as thralls?"

"They were never my people. I couldn't give a damn about any of them. Those women I sold to the east fetched a pretty coin, and the warriors they helped buy were worth knowing both your tribes suffered losses. I just wish the lot of you had been among them."

"Inga, you will not leave here alive. There is no reason to keep any secrets anymore. Freya and I set your women free and raided your riches hidden at this farm. Tell us what Grímr and Hakin have planned. Tell us what they will do next."

"Bah," she spat a glob of saliva at Erik's boots. "I will tell you nothing. You and your whore can go fuck yourselves."

Rangvald unlocked the cell door and was inside before Inga realized what was happening. He sliced through the bindings that kept her against the pole then grabbed her by the hair and shoved her face first into the wall. He allowed her only enough slack to turn her head before her face would have ground into the stonework.

"I've heard enough of your shite. My patience has grown tired with you. I was patient for the sake of you being my sister, but the woman I called sister died many years ago. I don't know who you are anymore, and so I feel no remorse treating you as I would a prisoner." He pulled her head back and slammed it against the wall. The stones cut into her temple and cheek, and Inga howled.

"Stop that wretched squawking or I will cut out your tongue." Rangvald shook her and pulled her back ready to bash her against the wall again when Inga jammed her foot down on his. Rangvald laughed at the woman's attempt to fight back. He drew a knife from his belt and held it to her throat as he kept her pinned. "You will die here, Inga. You can decide just how painfully you go to *hel*. Speak the truth, and I will make it swift. Test my patience further, and I will feel no guilt torturing you. Either way, you have no chance for mercy. Decide, woman."

Inga's maniacal laugh echoed until Rangvald drew the tip of his knife from the corner of her eye to her jaw and around to her chin. A slow trickle of blood flowed.

"Speak, woman."

Inga shook her head as much as her position allowed. Rangvald was far faster than she was and more experienced handling uncooperative captives. He shifted his hold on her and produced his war ax. He had her hand pressed flat on the wall before she saw the ax. Rangvald rested the blade against her fingers.

"What will it be, Sister?"

Inga held her tongue.

"Very well. One by one." Rangvald drew back the ax and struck her pinky which dropped to the ground. Blood squirted against the wall and dripped on the floor. "I will go until you have none left. On either hand. Then I shall take those hands off at the wrist. If you still refuse to talk, you will have no need for that tongue. I shall cut it out and feed it to the dogs. Then I will leave you here. You won't die from your wounds, but you will die slowly from dehydration when I refuse you food or drink. Test me, woman, and find out I'm not a man you should have underestimated."

Rangvald rested the blade against her ring finger, but Inga remained silent. That finger saw the same fate as her pinky. She trembled as the pain seared through her. Her knees shook, but she remained silent. She lost all the fingers on that hand before she relented.

"I will speak. *Nornar*, woman of fate that she is, must have decided at my birth that today would be the day of my death." She struggled to grind out any sound, but all four men heard her hoarse proclamation. "Grímr intends to allow Hakin to lead the fight. He plays the subordinate younger brother well. He lets Hakin lead the army, but it's to his advantage. He claims he leads the rear to keep them in order, but it's so he can back away if they must flee as they have many times. Hakin, fool that he is, believes Grímr is watching his back. Grímr will kill Hakin when he is no longer of use if one of you don't do it first. Grímr intends to defeat you both. He would replace the stronghold you burned. At first, he only wanted his own share of land with a homestead he could rule. Now we have nothing to go back to, he knows gaining more land is necessary but having people to work it is more important. He sees the potential for getting more than he ever expected. His greed grows with Hakin's ambition. Or perhaps it's the other way around. Either way, he intends to have both of your settlements for his own since there is nothing left for him to return to. Hakin thinks they will each have one of your villages, and they will rebuild the old one. Grímr does not think the same." Inga shrugged and fell silent.

"What is your part in all of this, Aunt Inga? Why the farm? Why are you helping them? You could have remained out of it and plead innocence, even said Einar forced you. Are you betraying Grímr and Hakin? Did they force you to sell the women?" Erik drilled her with questions.

Inga looked at each of the men.

"You still don't get it, do you? It's been me all along. I convinced Einar to switch his loyalties. I planted seeds of inferiority in Grímr's mind to get him to rise against Hakin. I bedded Hakin so he would feel superior to the little brother who is smarter and a better warrior, when he's willing to bloody his hands. I taunted Grímr by flirting with Hakin once Einar died. I reminded him he is nothing more than a gelding. I'm the one who decided we needed mercenaries. I created the idea in Hakin's mind and told him I knew of a way to pay them. Then I taunted Grímr but convinced him to buy the men's loyalty by paying them a bonus to switch allegiance. All the while I recouped that money by charging the men to bed my women. They could sleep with the whores before marrying them, but it cost them. They were more than willing. Some even took the women they chose to wife, but many moved on. That just meant they paid me back more of their wages."

Ivar, Leif, Rangvald, and Erik stood in disbelief. It was not impossible for them to picture a woman capable of plotting such a dastardly scheme. It shocked them that this woman, so connected to them, would hate them with such vengeance. Ivar and Leif knew they were the easy targets because of Ivar's past with Inga. But her hatred for her blood and the people she grew up with was more than any could conceive.

"So, what now?" Ivar asked.

"What do you mean? My being alive or dead will change nothing except Grímr and Hakin will need to find their money elsewhere. They're still determined to destroy both tribes and take both homesteads for themselves. Grímr still intends to kill Hakin and claim both for himself. One was to go to Tal, but now it will pass to our next son."

Rangvald still held her pinned against the wall. He slipped his bloodied ax back into his belt.

"Then you hold no remaining value to them," his hushed tones held menace.

"I suppose I don't," Inga agreed.

"Then you hold no value to us either." Rangvald drew his blade across her throat and let her body drop to the ground.

Erik stepped next to his father and placed his hand on his shoulder. Father and son looked at the woman who had been both sister and aunt. Neither could think of anything to say to one another or to the gods as her soul left her body and her eyes stared without seeing. Leif stepped to Erik's side and looked down at Inga. Ivar stood on Rangvald's other side.

"Rang, she chose the path of a *níðingr*, a shamed woman, and now she will make her home in the darkness and horror of *Náströnd* alongside Einar. They deserve each other as much in death as they did in life." Ivar knew there was little he could do to console his old friend, nor would the man want it. They could show no weakness. The dishonor of his sister's actions was bad enough without him appearing weak. He punished his sister as a jarl would. His mercy as her brother ended, but his duties as a jarl did not.

"Go to your wives," Leif offered. "We will see to her."

Rangvald and Erik stood still for a long moment before both turned towards the jarl's longhouse. At the door, they embraced.

"I'm sorry, Father. I wish it could have been different."

"As do I, Son. But that is not what fate decided. Or this is the consequence of other's believing they can control fate. As Inga said, the goddess of destiny chose this day for her when she was born. I just don't know that *Nornar* or fate planned this day to play out as it did." Rangvald pulled his son into his embrace once again.

"I couldn't be prouder of you." Rangvald cleared his throat as his emotions choked him. "You have grown into the man I saw in you as a boy. When *Nornar's* day comes for me and the Valkyries claim me, I thank the All Father for making you my son. You and Freya will lead our people to glory and prosperity. I love you, Erik. I couldn't imagine a better son than you. Your mother and I have been blessed with the family we dreamed of. You children are our legacy, and it is one I will rest in Valhalla knowing no one can ever destroy."

"Father, I am the man I am because you are the man I wanted to grow up to be. My brothers and sisters and I are fortunate to have you and Mother. We have seen what is to love and be loved. We have learned how to follow so we can lead. We are stronger for your love."

"Find your beautiful little bride and find solace in her arms. I will find mine with your mother."

Both men moved towards their chambers. Erik swiped his hand over his face and forced his shoulders to relax before pushing the door open.

Freya looked to the door as Erik stepped inside. Her smile radiated across the room and warmed the chill that settled in Erik's heart while listening to his aunt's ranting. Freya rose and stood before the fire. Erik sucked in a breath as he took in his wife's figure hidden by the linen tunic but outlined by the light behind her. She opened her arms to him, and he felt as though he floated across the space that separated them. They held one another in silence and absorbed the love that flowed between them. Erik buried his head in the crook of Freya's neck, and she ran a soothing hand through his hair. Erik wanted to carry his wife to their bed and sink inside her until he lost his mind to pleasure, but he needed to talk to her. He needed the comfort her ear could offer just as much as the comfort the rest of her body. He lifted her into his arms and lowered them in the chair Freya occupied while he was gone.

"I thought you might have fallen asleep by now. I didn't mean to be away so long."

Freya stroked his cheekbone before settling against his shoulder.

"I dozed, but I couldn't or rather wouldn't fall asleep until you returned. I needed to know you were all right." She slid her hand into the collar of his tunic and rubbed his chest.

"I'm sorry to have kept you up, but I am glad you're awake. There is so much to tell you, Freya. It didn't end well." Erik recounted the events and finished with the words he and his father exchanged. Through his story, Freya remained silent, but her hand roamed over his chest and shoulder offering him comfort. When he had nothing left to say, Freya slid from his lap. She took his hand and led him to the bed.

"I can't fix what she did. I can't make you unsee or unhear what you did tonight. I can't stop whatever Hakin and Grímr will do next. But I can make love to my husband. I can console you and ease your mind. I can distract you until we must both face reality again. I can show you my devotion by always being by your side."

Freya pulled the tunic over her head and let it fall to the ground as she slid onto the bed. She inched up and lifted her hair to cascade over the pillows. Erik's leather pants were snug as his half-hard rod turned to iron. He stripped off his clothes and climbed onto the bed and covered Freya with his body. Freya's knees fell wide as she accepted his body into hers. Their lovemaking was tender, more than it ever had been in the past. Erik's hips rocked with excruciating slowness. He circled them as he watched pleasure blossom on his wife's face. Freya wound her legs over his and wrapped her arms around his back.

"Let me feel all of you, Erik," she whispered.

Erik let his weight rest on her. He felt her share the burden both physically and spiritually. In that moment, more so than any leading up to it, he knew destiny and fate were real. It was why he found the perfect match to his soul and body. He brushed hair from Freya's temple and kissed it.

"I love you, Freya. May the gods forgive me for saying so, but I love you more than them and my life."

"If they are to smite you, then I shall go up in flames along with you for the same crimes. Erik, I love you, too." Freya arched her back as she felt the telltale tightening in her core.

"Erik," she breathed on a moan.

"Yes, my heart."

"The pennyroyal," she murmured. "I drank the tea tonight."

"Are you saying I can spill inside you."

"Yes," only her lips moved as her eyes slid shut.

The beauty of Freya's face mesmerized Erik as she moved beneath him. Her face was relaxed, and her lips were parted. She made quiet mewling sounds as her pleasure built to its climax. He watched as she crossed over and the spasms tightened around him.

"Look at me," he whispered.

Freya's eyes opened, and she took in the chiseled planes of his face.

"Gods you are the most beautiful man I have ever seen." She tangled her fingers into his hair as their mouths came together. Release crashed over and through them both as their kiss deepened. Even as the waves of climax abated, their kiss lingered. Erik reached behind him and pulled the covers over them. He had not noticed until then someone must have turned down the bed. Erik tried to roll them over, but Freya tightened her hold. He watched her shake her head, so he relented as she kissed a trail along his shoulder to his neck. They relaxed against one another, and both were asleep within a few more heartbeats.

CHAPTER TWENTY-ONE

Freya awoke to Erik tickling her side. The sun was already poking around the fur window covering when she rolled over.

"You sleep like the dead. Wake up, sleepyhead. If I'm going to enjoy the pleasures of my wife before the day begins, you need to wake up." Erik flicked her earlobe with his tongue.

"You know I don't, but there is something about sleeping next to you that relaxes me. I can't believe the sun is up."

"The sun and me." Erik nudged her, and she giggled as he continued to trail his fingernails along her ribs.

Freya rolled towards him and slid her leg over his hip. Her fingers curled around his cock as a pounding came at their door.

"Go away!" Erik barked.

"They're coming," Leif's voice floated through the door.

"At least someone is," Erik griped.

"We'll be there in a moment," Freya called as she rolled off the bed.

Erik reached for her but grasped only air before pounding his fist on the bed.

"I swear Loki is enjoying my suffering. We've been interrupted more times than not."

"All the more reason to hurry. We can kill Hakin and Grímr and get on with bedding one another without a battle disrupting things."

"Ever practical," Erik pouted.

They both hurried to dress and met everyone else outside. She moved to stand near Tyra. They spoke the night before but not for long enough.

"Are you ready for this?" Freya asked Tyra as the latter pulled on her bowstring testing its tautness.

"I am, but this old woman can't stop balking at everything I do," Tyra jerked her head in Bjorn's direction.

"And this overgrown child insists on running around as though her actions have no consequences." Bjorn stood with his hands on his hips glowering at Tyra.

Freya looked back and forth between her best friend and cousin.

"Still thinks your fates are joined?" she asked Tyra.

"They are," Bjorn cut in.

"They aren't," Tyra hissed. "And even if they were, I don't give a damn. You're a nag."

"And you're little more than a brat."

Freya walked away from the bickering and spotted Sigrid.

"What're you doing out here?" Freya jogged over to her. "Does Leif know you're outside?"

Freya scanned the area for her brother and spotted him with his back to them as he talked to their father.

"No, he'll make me go inside the moment he spots me. But I needed to find you. Freya, you must watch for Hakin. He will try to lose himself among his warriors when he can't find Grímr. He will end up next to you and Erik. You *must* fight him. Freya, it has to be you."

Freya looked at her sister-in-law and understood Sigrid was not making a suggestion.

"You've seen this." It was a statement not a question.

"I have."

"Sigrid!" Leif's bellow sounded like an angry bull about to charge.

"I have to go! Remember what I said. It's vital you fight him. Don't let him get away. The gods showed me it was you." Sigrid lifted her long tunic to her knees and ran as best as her belly would allow until she was inside the family's longhouse. Freya knew she would find shelter and safety in the hidden alcove where her own mother was waiting for Sigrid.

Freya looked for Erik. She would fight alongside him, and she knew Strian would pair with Tyra just as Leif and Bjorn paired. Erik waved her over to where he stood with both Rangvald and Lorna. Freya was yet to hear the story about Lorna and Rangvald. Freya intended to ask her mother-in-law how she came to be as well trained as Freya and Tyra, more so if Freya considered her added years of experience. Lorna was the most breathtaking woman she had ever seen, and dressed for battle with her hair pulled back, leather pants and leather vest, and a belt with several knives and an ax made her look like an avenging Valkyrie. She could imagine how Rangvald could have been so taken by her.

"Fight alongside me?" Erik asked when she came to stand beside him.

"Of course. Erik, Sigrid--" Freya was cut short by the sound of the battle horn.

En masse, Freya's tribe and those warriors Rangvald brought with him surged towards the gates of the wooden wall surrounding the homestead. They had the advantage of fighting downhill. Archers launched their arrows at the attackers who were beginning their ascent. Bodies began to litter the ground, and the enemy had to step over the fallen. Freya scanned the hoard for Grímr or Hakin, but could not find them. It was only moments later that pandemonium broke loose. The first contact was made between the combatants. Freya had only a moment to glance around and see her father fought as a trio with Leif and Bjorn, and as she suspected Strian paired with Tyra. She had a moment of panic as she realized the two most recently injured and still convalescing warriors were paired together. She pushed through the mass of fighters as she tried to make her way towards her family.

"Erik!" she called over her shoulder. "I need you this way."

She edged around two women but could not afford to look back to see if Erik followed. She made it only a few steps before she felt a large hand on her shoulder and sensed a large frame behind her. The gentleness of the touch was the only indicator it was Erik and kept her from brandishing her sword. She plowed on, reaching Strian and Tyra as the enemy surrounded them. She could see the effort Tyra made to hold her own as the woman's muscles flexed and strained. Strian kept up, but Freya could tell they each needed a partner who had more endurance. Paired with someone else, they would each stand the chance to defend themselves and overpower the enemies they faced.

"Bjorn! Leif! You must switch," she pulled away from Erik to take on the man approaching Tyra. "One of you to Tyra. The other to Strian."

Bjorn looked to her then Tyra. He saw Tyra struggle against a man a foot taller than she was, and while she was outmaneuvering him, Bjorn bellowed with rage. He slashed through two men to get to Tyra's side.

"I'm not dying today, woman, so you had better live." He received only a grunt in response.

Strian shifted and took Bjorn's spot with Leif and Ivar. Strian was now leaner than Leif or Ivar, and the less bulk made him more agile. He struck with his ax and knife whenever Leif or Ivar could create an indefensible area on the opponent's body.

"Freya!" Erik backed into her. "To my left, your right. Here come three."

Freya and Erik battled three against two, but after training together and fighting alongside one another through several skirmishes, they had an easy rhythm as two choreographed dancers. Movement to Freya's right signaled another warrior approaching. Her eyes shifted long enough to see it was Hakin, but he was not looking at her or Erik. He was not even looking at her family or friends. Instead he seemed to be searching for someone. Freya brought her sword down in a sharp sweep, taking the head off one opponent before thrusting forward into the other just as Erik ended the man he fought.

"Hakin's looking for someone, and it's not any of us."

"My parents?"

"Maybe. This way." Freya led the pair towards where Rangvald and Lorna fought. Freya had the briefest moment to wonder if she and Erik looked as synchronized as his parents. It was clear they knew each other's movements and intentions with no need for words. It was as if they were one beast with two heads and four arms. They moved as one.

"Impressive, aren't they?" Erik wiped sweat and blood from his face. "Don't worry. We are almost there."

Freya smirked, "Must you always read my mind?"

"Yes."

There was no time for more. Freya saw Hakin backing away as he tried to blend in while avoiding fighting. She scanned the area, but there was no sign of Grímr, but two warriors approached Erik and her. The shieldmaiden screeched as she launched herself at Freya, and the latter heard a man grunt as Erik's sword made impact with his opponent's shield. Freya focused on the woman in front of her. She was broader than Freya but quick; however, she had none of Freya's strength or agility. Freya taunted the woman as she moved out of reach or blocked the woman's thrusts. The quick burst of energy used by Hakin's shieldmaiden ran out, so it was only a few more swipes of her sword before Freya felled the larger woman. Freya swung around to help Erik and the two swords attacking at once was more than their opponent could defend.

"I have to find Hakin," Freya had to yell over the din of the nearby clashing swords.

"No. We fight where we are."

"You don't understand. I tried to tell you earlier. Sigrid told me I had to."

"Not yet. We can't move anywhere, and I don't see him."

Freya spun in a slow circle as she scanned for Hakin. Erik was right. The man was nowhere to be seen.

"What about Grímr? Have you seen him?"

Erik pointed his sword towards the dock.

"There. He hasn't joined the fight."

"Is he too injured or too coward? Or is he cunning enough to let his brother get himself killed?"

"The latter for sure."

Freya had no time to say anymore. She spotted Hakin making his way towards his brother. Hakin turned his back to Freya.

"Now," she called to Erik but did not wait for his response. She darted to the outskirts of the battle and pointed herself towards the docks. There were still mercenaries surging up the hill, but she dodged and skirted around them. Once again, she could not look behind her to see if Erik followed. She had to assume he would. Sigrid's prophecies came when they did for a reason. If Sigrid saw Freya slaying Hakin during this battle, Freya accepted this was fate's decision. She would not countermand the gods' decision.

One of Rangvald's men was locked in battle with Hakin, so it made it easy for Freya to position herself to strike. Rangvald's man spotted her, and she tilted her head away. The warrior backed away as Freya called out.

"I thought you were going to kill me and my brother. What about Erik Rangvaldson? You have all three of us here, yet you run away like a little girl who's wet her tunic."

Freya taunted Hakin knowing her words could not go unpunished. To insinuate Hakin was effeminate in any way was the gravest of insults to a Norseman. While taunting and insults were a common tactic in battle, her choice of words went beyond the norm.

"Did Inga steal your cock the last time you plowed her? She seemed in control when I saw her."

Hakin roared with fury and charged forward. His retreat forgotten and his pride injured, he attacked like an injured boar. Freya was prepared. She blocked his first swing, and the reverberation seared through her arm all the way to her ribs, but she struck out her leg and kicked him in the abdomen. He stumbled back several feet, and Freya used it to her advantage. She brought her sword up over her left shoulder as she held it in both hands and hacked straight down. Her blade sliced through Hakin's sword arm at the elbow. Blood erupted from the severed limb, and Hakin stood frozen looking at the stump and then the forearm and hand that lay on the ground. Freya watched the transformation as he moved from an angry warrior to a berserker. She knew what to expect. He pulled a knife from his belt and once again charged her. Despite the blood spewing from his wound, he moved like a man possessed. He thrust his knife towards her throat, but she twisted her wrist and rammed the hilt of her sword into his nose. She hoped to shove the bone straight back into his brain, but the angle of impact only broke it. More blood spurted from him, and he crumpled to the ground. She took a step forward to end Hakin's life, but a hand grabbed a fistful of her vest and yanked her backwards taking her off her feet. She tried to twist, but she realized Erik pulled her away just as one of Hakin's men stood poised to decapitate her.

"I will take you over my knee later, and it won't be for either of our pleasure." Erik was angrier than Freya had ever heard him. She knew he would be within his rights as her husband, and he was entitled to demand punishment for a partner who abandoned him during battle.

"Yes, husband." It was the most deferential she had ever heard herself be, and it was the most deferential she ever felt.

Erik's response was a grunt as he continued to drag her away from the fighting.

"Wait. Erik, he's not dead."

"And neither are you."

"I have to make sure. I have to kill him. Sigrid said so."

"But did Sigrid also tell you to leave me with no clue where you were running to? Did Sigrid tell you to stand there and get your head lopped off? I'm sure she didn't."

Freya saw Erik's body tremble with anger. His eyes were the color of glaciers that broke off and floated through the fjords. A frozen blue and directed at her.

"Erik," she choked.

"Don't. Not now. We will deal with this later."

Erik turned away, and that's when she saw the gash that ran along the back of his ribs to just below his arm.

"Erik," she screamed. "Dear gods, you're injured."

"I know," his withering glare made the bile rise in her throat.

She could not move. Remorse, guilt, shame, and fear froze her in place.

When she did not follow him again, Erik looked back and watched as Freya's heart broke. It was as though he could see through her to the shards splintering apart.

"It's not that bad. More of a graze."

"But I did that. I'm as guilty as if it were my blade. I got you injured, and I could have gotten you killed."

The battle swirled on around them. The noise of hundreds of swords clanging, the screams of pain, and grunts of effort were deafening. The injured and dead strewn the ground. The stench of death and defecation was nauseating. But all Freya could take in was the danger she put her husband in, and the disappointment in herself for failing him.

"I'm angry, not because I got injured but because I couldn't defend you. You did what you wanted to do never mind the risk it put you in. That's what infuriates me. But Freya, I'm not leaving you."

Freya swallowed but shook her head.

"You have every right to."

"No, I don't. You are a warrior first in battle, and my wife second. You did what we train a warrior to do. It's me who is having a hard time not being a husband first then a warrior. I'm angry as your partner that you risked both our lives, but I won't stop loving my wife over it. Now, can we please go?"

Erik grabbed her wrist and pulled her back up the hill. She looked over her shoulder and saw a man pulling Hakin towards their boats. She could not tell if he was alive or dead.

"Erik." He looked back at her, and he followed her sword as she pointed out Hakin. "What if he's not dead?"

"Then he will be soon. There is no way he could survive the amount of blood he was losing."

"But you can't be sure."

"No, I can't. But I can be sure we must continue fighting."

As if on cue, four mercenaries materialized and surrounded them. Their conversation was over.

CHAPTER TWENTY-TWO

They spent the remainder of the morning in battle. Hakin had more of his own tribe's warriors than anyone expected, and then there were the mercenaries he and Grímr hired. Five boats sailed into the fjord. Three were the ones that followed them from Scotland, even after one disappeared, and the other two must have met them along the way, explaining the delay. The mercenaries might have been useless sailors, but they were all well-trained fighters. Most fought in their plaids, but none of them wore clan colors, favoring solid black or dark blue. It was still impossible to tell which clan was supporting Hakin or Grímr, or, if not supporting them, at least had plenty of men willing to fight. Freya knew the men from Orkney because they wore leather breeches like the Norse. They blended in with Hakin's tribe, but many favored the longer Highland broadsword.

It was not a decisive victory, not with hundreds of casualties and deaths on both sides, but the enemy was forced to retreat. With Hakin too injured to fight or lead, and Grímr refusing to engage beyond the middle of the hill, they retreated once more to the boat. Erik surmised that Grímr remained positioned midway up the hill to ostensibly support those in the rear or to prevent them retreating without the signal. Everyone was sure Grímr did not engage because he did not want to endanger himself and risk not outlasting everyone else. His goal was still to be jarl of Hakin's, Rangvald's and Ivar's homesteads, a goal he could not achieve if he was dead.

Freya and Erik made their way to her parents' longhouse with all the others. They walked beside one another without speaking, but just before they entered, Erik pulled Freya aside.

"We're going straight to our chamber. Grab clean clothes and your soap."

Freya looked at Erik and saw none of the anger from earlier. Instead she saw the same weariness she felt. She nodded her head, and they went to their chamber. Freya hurried to gather what she needed. The last thing she wanted was to keep Erik waiting. They exited the longhouse but did not get far before they heard Sigrid call to Freya. They walked back to meet as she held her belly and hurried towards them.

"Freya, you took his sword arm, didn't you?"

Freya nodded but looked to the ground.

Sigrid looked between the couple and stepped forward to place her hands on both Freya's shoulders.

"Look at me, Freya. You took an enormous risk today. One I didn't mean for you to take when I said it had to be you to slay Hakin. I should have been clearer and not put so much pressure on you." Sigrid looked to Erik. "It's my fault she took off on her own. I stressed the importance she not let Hakin get away. I insisted it had to be her. I saw it all. But I didn't see the danger Freya was in until another vision came during the battle. However, I know you didn't kill him here, but he dies before the night is through. You have rid us of one of our evils."

Freya did not move. Erik and Sigrid watched her, but her eyes remained on the ground. The cousins looked at one another, and Sigrid's expression made it clear she expected him to take care of his wife. Sigrid turned back to the longhouse, and Erik scooped Freya into his arms. She curled into his chest and rested her head on his shoulder.

"I told you, princess, one day you would enjoy me carrying you. Do you remember that?"

Freya nodded but said nothing.

"You didn't like me very much back then."

"Not true," she whispered. "I loved you. I didn't enjoy thinking you believed I was weak."

Erik pulled the door to the bathhouse open as he balanced Freya. They stepped inside the warm wooden building. Erik put Freya down and moved to the bucket of water that sat near the wall. He scooped a ladle full to pour over the hot stones in the center. Steam rose and filled the air, and Erik walked over to open the hatch in the wall that would allow water from the hot spring to enter one tub. The tub would warm too once Erik lit the small fire pit below it.

Freya listlessly watched Erik move about as he prepared a bath. She felt too drained to assist him. She knew it was not battle fatigue but the emotional strain of waiting to see how Erik would punish her. She felt anxious and agitated but too worn out for her body to show it. Erik returned and undressed her. His touch was slow and gentle as he released the buttons on her fur vest and pushed it from her shoulders. He pulled her tunic loose from the waist of her breeches but paused.

"Freya, are you scared?"

She looked into eyes she recognized once again. The warmth had returned, but she was still frightened. She was his wife now, and he had the right to do as he saw fit in punishing her. She had angered him plenty of times before, perhaps not as much as she had that day, but he had never lain a hand on her. She nodded once.

"Oh, Freya." She heard the frustration in his voice and took a step back. "Stop."

She froze.

"Freya, I was furious with you. We both know that. I told you it was the risk you put yourself in that angered me, but it was also my inability to stop you or protect you. We failed each other today. You abandoned me to fight alone, but I failed you by not following soon enough."

Erik released the clasp to his fur cloak and pulled his tunic over his head. He saw Freya watching him, saw the spark of desire, and then watched it fizzle as shame replaced it. He lifted her chin and tried to read the storm of emotions brewing within her eyes.

"I know you feel remorse for me getting injured, which you can see is just a scratch," he twisted to show her. "And I know you feel shame for not being there. And I think you feel you've dishonored yourself. But what I don't understand is whether you're afraid I will punish you or if you're afraid I will leave you. Which do you fear?"

"Both."

Erik drew in a deep breath before proceeding.

"I spoke out of anger and my own fear earlier. I will never lay a hand on you in anger. Never. That doesn't mean there won't be times, as your husband, where I'm within my rights to punish you. But that doesn't mean I will. We are partners. You are not a child, and you are not my property. You are free to make your own choices even when I don't agree with them. If I put you over my knee and spank you, I promise it will most definitely be for both of our pleasure."

Freya's eyes widened, and Erik saw a spark of interest before it once again snuffed out.

"I'm also not leaving you. Do you have any idea how my parents argue? You are more like my mother than I realized until today. They have had the same issue more than once in battle. Except, in fairness to my mother, it's not always her charging off. I wouldn't be surprised if they aren't arguing over it right now. But my parents love each other far more than the anger either of them might temporarily harbor. I pledged myself to you, and I meant it. I won't turn my back on you. But don't retreat from me either."

Erik struggled to push out the final words as emotion choked him. Freya heard the catch in his voice and reached out a tentative hand. Erik grasped it and placed it over his heart.

"But I dishonored myself by not keeping my pledge to always be by your side."

Erik grinned.

"Did you mean that pledge literally? I pray not. I prefer to use the chamber pot alone. That's not something I want you to see."

"You know that's not what I meant," Freya huffed.

"But apparently, it is. You have always been by my side since we met. We have partnered many times, and I trust you implicitly as my wife to continue as my partner. Just because we didn't fight together the entire time doesn't mean you were disloyal to me."

"You could have died," Freya blurted out. "It would have been my fault. It may as well have been my sword plunged into you."

Erik pulled her into his embrace and stroked her hair.

"Don't you think I feel the same guilt. How do you think I felt when I realized you were no longer there, and I'd failed to notice? You told me you needed to go after Hakin, so I should have known you'd look for the opportunity. You could have died too. Don't you think I would feel it was my fault? I shouldn't have spoken out of anger and threatened you. My poor choice of words isn't worth the agony you are putting yourself through."

Freya wrapped her arms around his waist. She closed her eyes and absorbed the comfort Erik's presence offered. It settled her in a way no one else could. She thought back over the many heated words she had thrown at him in the months since they met. She cringed as she realized her callous and spiteful comments were often far worse than her husband's.

"It's no small miracle that not only do you put up with me, but you keep coming back for more."

"What?"

"I was just thinking about some of the worst things I've said to you over the past three moons. I was not nice to you. Many times. I don't know where you get your patience from."

"My mother. Have you met my father and my brothers?"

"You must care for me."

Erik leaned back, and Freya looked up at him.

"More than I could ever express with words or my body. I am not without my faults too. I know how fortunate I am to have you love me. You could have had your choice of any man in the Trondelag, but you chose me."

"Always. And I will over and over."

Their kiss was filled with need. It was only moments later that they scattered their clothes on the floor.

Freya's and Erik's tribe members gathered around the large altar at twilight. Someone led a goat forward, and the shaman lifted it high into the air reciting the ancient rituals before slaughtering it. Erik and Freya joined hands as they recited their vows before their friends and families. Rangvald stepped forward with the sword Erik would give to Freya for their future son. She presented him with a jewel encrusted knife and the rings they would exchange. As the vows ended and the shaman called upon the gods to make them fruitful, Erik and Freya kissed for the first time as a legally married couple though in their eyes they married days ago. They grinned at one another as the crowd cheered around them.

"This is so much better than if we had waited. I'm glad you insisted that we marry before the sun rose again. I was not looking forward to digging through old bones to find that sword," Erik's hushed tones did not even reach the shaman who still stood near them.

"I'm glad I insisted too."

After they finished bathing, the couple sought their parents and threatened to sneak away with the shaman soon if their families insisted on the ancient rituals. They were not interested in Erik retrieving a buried sword to prove his manhood or Freya being scrubbed of her innocence, which everyone knew she lost years ago. Both sets of parents knew their child well enough to know it was no empty threat, so they arranged the ceremony for that evening.

Erik lifted Freya into his arms and turned towards the jarl's longhouse.

"Don't protest, princess. I like the feel of you in my arms."

"I wasn't going to. I was going to make today the first time I asked you to carry me. You said I eventually would."

Erik let go of Freya so unexpectedly she almost fell. He stood with his arms crossed as she righted herself. Her eyes widened as her hands went to her hips.

"Well?" Erik questioned.

"Well, what?"

"Today? Now? She's really going to pick an argument with him now?" Bjorn called.

"It's not me. He tried to drop me. Arrogant son of a pig farmer."

"I thought we agreed you wouldn't call my father names anymore."

Freya's eyes sparked as she took in the broad chest and the muscles that flexed as he crossed his arms. She looked at the angular jaw and sharp nose she both wanted to hit and kiss.

"I would say my son is to blame for antagonizing her."

"Thank you, Mother," Erik grumbled. "You said you would ask me to carry you. I wanted to hear it."

"You should have thought about my reactions before you dropped me."

"I didn't drop you."

"You didn't set me down gracefully either."

Erik and Freya grinned at one another. Their banter was playful this time. Freya leaned forward and placed her hands on his crossed arms as she stretched to whisper in his ear.

"Will you carry me to bed now?"

Erik's arms fell away, and he pulled her in for a kiss that had the crowd cheering. She was back into his arms before her next breath. He marched them into the main room of the longhouse and snatched a pitcher of mead from the table before spinning toward their chamber.

"Interrupt us on pain of death," Erik called over his shoulder as he kicked the door shut to their chamber.

EPILOGUE

"Erik, wake up." Freya nudged Erik several times before he opened his eyes. The chamber was dark, and he could not even make out his wife's form, but he felt her moving off the bed.

"What is it? Is it the babe?"

"Yes, but not ours. I think Sigrid's time has come."

Freya struggled to pull a tunic over her rounded belly. It seemed like every time she tried to get dressed, she found another article of clothing that was too snug. Erik lit a torch from the embers of the fire.

"Where are you going? You should be in bed resting. You had pains all day too."

"Stop whittling. The midwife said they were only practice pains. I'm going to see Sigrid."

"Freya," his voice warned.

"Erik," her voice mimicked.

"You are the singularly most frustrating woman All Father put on this earth."

"And he did it just for you."

Erik pulled his wife into his embrace. While her belly now made it difficult for her to wrap her arms around his waist, his arms were still long enough to clasp her to his chest.

"Promise me you will come back to rest if your pains start again."

Freya mumbled her response against his chest.

"Promise if you're in pain, you'll come back, Freya, or I'll keep you here."

"Fine," she pecked his cheek. "But you know you couldn't keep me here."

"Don't test me, woman."

"I love you too."

Freya slipped from their room and moved down the corridor to the one Sigrid and Leif shared with their two-year-old son Thorson. Before she opened the door, she heard Sigrid cry out in pain. Freya rubbed a hand over her own belly and back trying to ease the knots that kept coming and going. She knew she would be next. She only hoped the midwife would be done with Sigrid by the time Freya needed her. Freya saw Tyra approaching, and they entered Sigrid's chamber together. They found Leif pacing and shooting looks of panic at Sigrid. It tempted Freya to tease Leif, but she knew Erik would be far worse by morning.

It was not much longer before Sigrid was delivering her daughter, and Freya was slipping back into her chamber. Erik sat in the chair by the fire but rose when he saw her.

"How is she? How're they?"

"I think Leif was in more agony than Sigrid," she giggled as she looked at her enormous husband who she knew would be reduced to the same nervous mess her brother had just been. "Sigrid is well, and the babe is being delivered now."

Erik walked to Freya and rubbed her lower back. She leaned against him for support.

"How're you?"

"I'm going to need you to fetch the midwife as soon as she's done with Sigrid."

"What? Freya, what happened? What's wrong?" Erik lifted her and carried her to the bed. He lowered her to the mattress as though she was the most fragile treasure he had ever touched. To him, she was.

"Nothing is wrong, and the only thing that happened is my labor pains are now much closer together."

"Closer? Not started but closer. You've been having them all along." It was a terse statement not a question. "You promised to return here if you were in pain."

"I wasn't in pain until all of a sudden I was in pain." She knew that only made sense to her. "They were uncomfortable before, but now--" A contraction stole her breath.

Erik was out the door before it banged against the wall. Moments later, he was pushing the old woman who served as the tribe's midwife into the chamber.

"It's too soon. We only came here for Sigrid's delivery. We were supposed to make it home before it was Freya's time." Erik's voice rose with each word.

"Stop working yourself into a lather, my boy," the old woman patted his arm. "Go be useful. Help get your wife comfortable."

Tyra and Lorna entered a moment later and helped Erik get Freya situated.

"You're not needed now. We will let you know when your babe is here," the midwife tried to shoo Erik from the chamber, but his responding growl was feral.

He climbed onto the bed next to Freya and helped her lean forward, so he could slide in behind her. They spent the next few hours with Freya alternating between crushing Erik's hands and resting her head against his solid shoulder. When Freya thought she had no more to give, Erik coaxed her into pushing three more times, and their son arrived. Mother and father looked bewilderedly at one another before Freya reached out for their baby, and Erik supported the newborn's head as Freya placed him to her breast.

"I'm so proud of you, Freya." He kissed her temple.

"Look what we made together." She whispered as she marveled at their son's strength when his tiny fingers curled around her thumb. She brushed the tiny hand against her lips.

"What shall you call him?" Lorna asked.

"Reinhold Erikson," Freya beamed.

"That's a fine name," Tyra grinned. "And not one we were considering."

Tyra rubbed her own swollen belly as she chuckled.

"I need to get back before my husband worries himself into an early grave. Worse than an old woman. But he loves me, and I love him."

Lorna approached the bed as Tyra left.

"I'm proud of you, Erik. Your father is too. He is excited to meet his first grandchild. He'll come by in the morning. Enjoy your time as a new family."

Lorna kissed each of their cheeks and brushed the back of her finger against her grandson's cheek.

"I love you, Erik."

"I love you, Freya."

The new parents gazed upon their precious creation, and both cherished every moment that led up to this.

THANK YOU FOR READING FREYA

Celeste Barclay, a nom de plume, lives near the Southern California coast with her husband and sons. Growing up in the Midwest, Celeste enjoyed spending as much time in and on the water as she could. Now she lives near the beach. She's an avid swimmer, a hopeful future surfer, and a former rower. When she's not writing, she's working or being a mom.

Visit Celeste's website, www. celestebarclay. com, for regular updates on works in progress, new releases, and her blog where she features posts about her experiences as an author and recommendations of her favorite reads.

Are you an author who would like to guest blog or be featured in her recommendations? Visit her website for an opportunity to share your insights and experiences.

Have you read *Leif, Viking Glory Book One*? Learn how the saga begins!

Do the Highlands call to your heart? *Their Highland Beginning, The Clan Sinclair Prequel* will introduce you to Celeste's first series. This FREE novella is available to all new subscribers to Celeste's monthly newsletter. Subscribe on her website.

Join all the fun and receiving insider information about new releases and giveaways when you join Celeste Barclay's Ladies of Yore Facebook Group

www. celestebarclay. Com
www.facebook.com/groups/celestebarclaysladiesofyore

FREE WHEN YOU SIGN UP FOR CELESTE'S NEWSLETTER!

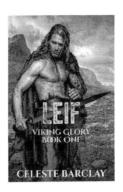

LEIF VIKING GLORY BOOK ONE

Fate brought them together. Free will binds them.

Leif Ivarrson wants nothing more than to enjoy the comforts of home after sailing for months. When a neighboring jarl arrives bearing news of a threat to their land and security, Leif knows there will be no rest for him. Tasked with finding and bringing back this jarl's niece, Leif departs on a journey that fate designed but he chooses to carry out.

Sigrid Torbensdóttir's visions have been both a gift and a curse since she was a young girl. Now a woman, Sigrid's position as a seer puts her in danger when enemies seek to take advantage of her gift for their benefit and to keep her from saving her family. Sigrid knows she cannot defy fate, and when Leif comes to her rescue, Leif discovers destiny cannot be ignored.

Leif and Sigrid struggle to reconcile the future the gods have shown her with the shifting fate their enemies attempt to control.

Will a new love survive the tests of war and family? Can a match created by fate withstand the machinations of man?

Purchase or download on Amazon and Barnes and Noble
www.books2read.com/leifvikingglory1

HIS HIGHLAND LASS THE CLAN SINCLAIR, BOOK 1

An undeniable love... an unexpected match... Faced with a feud with the Sinclairs that is growing deadly, Laird Tristan Mackay is bound by duty to his clan to make peace with the enemy. Tristan arranges a marriage for his stepbrother, Sir Alan, but never imagines that he would meet the woman he longs to marry. When things sour quickly between Tristan's stepbrother and Lady Mairghread Sinclair, Tristan is determined to make her his. A choice that promises to change his life forever.

Raised with four older warriors for brothers and as the only daughter of the Sinclair laird, Mairghread is independent resourceful, and loyal to her family. Mairghread is betrothed to one man but it is the dark, handsome, and provocative laird who catches her eye.

Neither of Tristan nor Mairghread imagined they would find the passion that grows between them. However, a spurned mistress and a jilted suitor stand between Tristan and Mairghread's happiness.

Destined for another... Mairghread Sinclair is not prepared for the danger that awaits her while visiting the Mackay clan. She must use her wits to keep herself alive when danger pulls her away from the man she loves.

Fated to be together... Laird Tristan Mackay was not looking for a wife, but could Lady Mairghread Sinclair be the one to open his heart and bring peace to their clans, or will their passion tear the two clans apart?

Purchase or download on Amazon and Barnes & Noble www.books2read.com/hishighlandlass

Made in the USA
Lexington, KY
20 June 2019